The old man had a sword, but it was still sheathed. He stood quietly in the middle of the circling Ronin, silent and unruffled.

Then the Ronin stopped circling. One raider advanced, his sword raised, his mouth open in screaming anticipation of the slaughter.

Without looking to the right or left, the old man's head snapped up. At the same instant he drew his weapon. In and out the blade flicked, and the howling changed to a choked gurgle. Now his sword swept around leftward from behind, slicing through the ribs of the raider there. Now it turned in mid-air, reversing its sweep, and another raider met death as the blade swept under his guard. As the sword had flicked in, it flicked back out, catching the closest man in the throat. A quick step, a final thrust, and the last of the killers lay gurgling out his life in the clearing.

The old man cleaned his blade with a mighty sweep of his sword, a sweep which spatted blood and flesh in a centrifugal fountain of gore. Then, with a deft movement, he returned it to its scabbard and stood quietly gazing at the huddled bodies surrounding him.

"You may approach. They are all dead," he said to Jerome.

WAY-FARER

by

DENNIS SCHMIDT

ace books
A Division of Charter Communications Inc.
A GROSSET & DUNLAP COMPANY
360 Park Avenue South
New York, New York 10010

WAY-FARER

An ACE Book

Cover art by Ben Venuti

First Ace printing: June 1978

Printed in U.S.A.

PROLOGUE

Something's got to be wrong. It's just too damn perfect! *Paul Suarez leaned on his shovel, let his gaze pass over the gently rolling hills to the distant mountains, purple in the slight haze.*

No question about it, it's the most beautiful sight I've ever seen: oh, sure, the light's a little bluer than Sol's, and the vegetation's a bit queer—but these are little things. *He'd been, he knew, conditioned to absorb much greater stresses.*

So what could it be? Why do I feel so uneasy? *A shadow swept over him. He looked up quickly: more of the one-way orbit-to-ground airfoil type transports, with their loads of Pilgrims and their meager possessions. The transports would slip gently to earth not far from where he was working, there to be unloaded and then dismantled to supply building components for Base. As he watched, a bigger, multiple-use type shuttle came to a roaring touch-down farther off in a separate area already blackened by exhaust flames.*

1

That must be about the last load. Even the kids are down. Nobody left in orbit except for the Flagship's Command Staff—and the Admiral, of course. They must still be re-checking the Planetary Analysis data brought in by the probes and survey teams. *They had been 95 percent sure before they'd let even the first landing party go down, 99 percent before they'd dispatched the Main Survey. Before the first load of Pilgrims had debarked that "99" had been carried to four decimal places. But the Admiral was still checking, and would continue to do so until the Flagship left its parking orbit for the return trip to Earth. Suarez knew all this.*

So why do I feel this way? Kensho has no intelligent native life, nor any animal remotely dangerous to an armed man. No inimical micro-organisms. No weird proteins. It's like somebody had set out to create the perfect planet for human colonization . . . or the perfect trap. Death wears many beautiful masks . . .

For the Virgin's sake, stop! This is not the slums of Ciudad—this is Kensho, a new planet. *Your* new planet! For you the rat-infested ruins of Earth no longer exist. You've escaped; you're free! Your children will grow up proud and strong, and their children, and their children's children. Be happy, idiot!

But somewhere in the back alleys of his mind a cynical little voice chuckled: "You may not get what you pay for," it whispered, "but you always pay for what you get. Did not all your years in the street teach you that there is no such thing as a free lunch?"

Jesu! Basta! Silence! *The voice snickered quietly.*

"Sure beats that damn cesspool, Earth, eh, Mex?" commented a gruff voice beside him. Startled, Suarez turned his head to find Wes Bannerman leaning on another shovel. *"Yeh,"* he replied laconically, not really in the mood for conversation.

Bannerman had no such reluctance; he obviously wanted to talk. *"Damn, but I'm sure glad I joined the Pilgrimage! She-it, hombre, now I got a chance to do all the things I always wanted to do! You know what? First thing they get the animals quickened and matured, I'm gonna apply for a horse. They brought 'em—I saw the manifest while we were unloading the zygotes. And when I get my horse I'm gonna make me a saddle and ride across those hills, like a goddamn Texan should! This colony's gonna need explorers, and I'm gonna be one or know why!*

"By God, Mex, don't you laugh—I mean it! It's something I've dreamed of all my life." Suarez smiled in spite of his dark mood. Bannerman's rough good humor and enthusiasm were contagious.

Hell, Texas is damn near as bad as Ciudad. It took quite a few hits during the Co-Dominium War. Mostly slagged rubble and desert now. Yet look at Bannerman. The big loco jerk is as excited as a kid. Rarin' to go, not wasting any energy worrying about how good things have turned out, just accepting his luck and riding with it.

The big Texan straightened up and looked over at Suarez out of the corner of his eye, uncertainly, with a quality almost of coyness that would have been hilarious were it not so touching. "You'd . . . uh . . . maybe you'd like to ride with me, amigo?"

For a moment Suarez continued to gaze out over the hills. "Hell," he finally said, "maybe I would." He turned to look directly at Bannerman.

Why don't I hate this gringo? He calls me "Mex" all the time, and he uses pidgin Spanish whenever he talks to me . . . but he doesn't seem to mean anything bad by it—it seems to be his way of showing affection. I think he wants to be my friend.

Friend. It was a new idea to Suarez. One didn't have friends in the teeming warrens of Ciudad. It was every man for himself, and root, hog, or die. Friend . . . It made him feel good and strange at the same time.

Bannerman held out his hand. "Compadre, I'd be proud to have you." Suarez took the hand and shook it.

"Well," the big man turned back to his shovel, "guess we better quit the jawbonin' and start diggin' muy pronto or that damn Looie will be over here beatin' out chingas." Suarez glanced over his shoulder and nodded. Bannerman continued, his words matching the rhythm of his work. "Don't know why . . . the Admiral couldn't . . . let us use . . . lasers . . . for this damn job . . . what'd it hurt? . . . gonna hafta work . . . hard enough . . . once the Flagship leaves . . . deserve a little help now . . . you know . . . break us in . . . gradual like . . ."

Murmuring token agreement, Suarez dug stead-

ily. Bannerman knew as well as he did why Admiral Nakamura was making them set up Base with hand tools. Once the Flagship left, the Pilgrims on Kensho would be without the advanced technology of Earth. Oh, they'd have a basic industrial capacity of their own, the ability to manufacture the simple tools and implements needed for their spread over Kensho. But they were destined to be an agricultural society for many generations to come.

When they were ready they'd build their own technology, based on the information stored in the Central Library here at Base. For now, though, the Laws of the Pilgrimage demanded that they prepare themselves for the kind of lives they and their children would be living. And they'd be digging with shovels for a long time to come.

Suarez stopped and leaned on his shovel again.

What was that? Maybe I'm working too hard. There it was again! *A strange tingling feeling, almost like heat, at the edge of his mind.*

Odd. Maybe the sun. *The feeling came stronger, in a great wave. He stood, looked wildly about.*

I need help! *Others were also standing.* Oh, my God—the lunch isn't free after all!

Bannerman looked up. "Hey, Mex, you OK?"

Mex! That hated slur again! Fucking Gringo spitting on la Raza! Hijo de puta! Filthy Texan bastard! Always giving me all kinds of shit, spouting rotten Spanish! Jesus how I hate that pedaze de carraco! Hate him! HATE HIM! HATE!

Screaming, Suarez split his friend's skull with the blade of his shovel.

5

****

(background of hunger hunger hunger hunger)
Flicker of awareness
Tentative search
Energy source!
Alertness of totality.

Viable energy source!
Quantity?   Extensive and growing.
Quality?   Súperior.
Decision of totality:
     Gather and await full
     realization of potential. Acceptance.
(gather gather gather gather gather gather)
               TOTALITY UNIFIED
          Period of waiting.
Analysis of potential. Judgement. Decision.
          Attack! Attack!
               Feed!!!
               Feed!
               Feed.
     Satiation. Quiessence.
     Awareness of status.
      Quantity of source seriously diminished.
               Concern.
Viability endangered? Possibility.
          Recall of previous experience:
          Source attacked.
               Viability destroyed.
               Source destroyed.
               Hungerhungerhunger . . .
               Totality diminished.
  DANGER!
               Problem.   Grave concern.
Solution?   Withdraw.   Wait.

****

The whole area was littered with corpses. Here and there a body writhed in its final death throes, or a drooling, jibbering hulk shambled insanely by, while a few stunned survivors huddled off to one side, clinging to each other for mutual support against the horror of the scene. In a far corner, one last dying killer was tearing at the throat of another.

Admiral Y. Nakamura, Commander of the Flagship Mushima, Leader of the Pilgrimage Expedition, High Master of the Universal Way of Zen, switched off the hologram and sat back with a sigh. It was his twelfth time through the scene. Unpleasant, but necessary.

He sat alone in the Command Conference Room aboard the Flagship, which hung in synchronous orbit directly over First Touch. His crew and officers had been sent down to organize relief for the survivors of the attack, and to gather information.

So far, he had reached several conclusions. First, whatever had decimated the Pilgrims at Base was either invisible or microscopic. He had viewed the event in everything from infra-red to ultra-violet light and found no sign of the attacker. A vastly enlarged projection had been equally unproductive, nor had a scrutiny of the records of the ship's other sensors turned up anything of interest.

Forced to choose between an invisible enemy or a microscopic one, he chose the latter and checked the autopsy reports on several of the victims. There was no sign of any foreign body, cellular, viral, or chemical. Indeed, the only unusual thing about the dead Pilgrims was that their systems were flooded with adrenalin and the synapses of some of their neurons appeared to have "burned out," as if overloaded. He had never heard of such a thing and had no idea what it could mean.

Reluctantly returning to the alternate theory—that the source of the attacker was invisible—he realized his only source of information would be the actions of the men who had experienced it. He ran the hologram through twice more at normal speed, then slowed it down considerably, especially the opening sequences.

In creeping slow motion, he watched a calm Pilgrim turn into a raving beast. He could see the first shock, the fear, the growing, upward-spiraling surge of horror that finally exploded into madness. Again and again, he watched the same process unfold in other victims.

Having discovered the similarities, he began searching for differences. The first that caught his eye was the time differential in the passage from calmness to insanity in each individual. Some seemed literally to erupt. Others appeared to be able to fight it off for a time.

Then he remembered the survivors. Quickly he ran the hologram to the end, identified one of those who had not succumbed, and followed that individual backwards to the opening sequence. Intently, from the beginning, he watched that face. There was the same initial fear. But what followed was not increasing terror. Rather there was a brow-wrinkling, sweat-producing effort to fight back, to control the emotions, to get hold of one's self! A cross-check on other survivors produced confirmation.

Sure of what he would find, Nakamura punched up the psych-profiles of the survivors and a random sample of those who had died. Even a quick survey showed what he had suspected: to a man, those who had beaten off the attack had stable, strong personalities. Curious, he cross-tabulated the data in terms of religious affiliation. The result was revealing: 50% of the members of sects which practiced mind control had lived through the attack, against 14% for other groups. Only one follower of the Universal Way of Zen had died, a pickaxe sunk eight inches into his neck.

Nakamura's third conclusion was now obvious. Whatever it was, it affected men's minds. It started small, apparently working within the mind on whatever emotional instability was present. It grew rapidly, perhaps enhancing the existing instability by feeding it back into the mind in an ever-increasing spiral of emotion. If the individual did not clamp down on it with iron control, he would quickly be driven into raving madness.

He sighed again and rubbed his temples with tired fingers. He had learned all he would learn by reviewing the past. Precious little it was, too! Now it was time to bring himself up to date on the current situation. His officers would have had time to beam up their respective reports by now. If he needed more data, he could probably ferret it out of the ship's computer.

Within an hour, he knew the worst. About 80% had perished in the first attack. Things were temporarily quiet, but it was clear that the assault could be renewed at any moment. Given the condition of the survivors, he doubted any would be able to withstand the shock. There was no way he could organize a defense since he only knew what the enemy did, not what it was. Hence the only sensible choice was to cut and run for it.

Which was impossible. The fatality rate among the crew and officers who had been present at First Touch when the attack struck, and had been caught in the middle trying to stop the slaughter, had been even higher than among the Pilgrims. There were barely enough men left to man the Flagship, let alone the four Arks.

In addition, the vehicles that had taken the Pilgrims down had been one-way transports with just enough fuel capacity to enter atmosphere safely and make minor course corrections; once grounded they could never fly again. And all but one of the heavy-duty shuttles had been planetside at the time. They all had sustained heavy damage and would require extensive repairs before they could be made spaceworthy. He had neither the engineers to do the work nor the time in which to do it. And even if he had both, there was insufficient fuel to evacuate more than a third of the survivors.

So he couldn't run.

And he couldn't stay.

A logical analysis of the problem indicated that the answer was a-logical. So much for Aristotle! So much for Science, too, he mused. Even before the third Probe had returned, the planet had rated over 97%. At the time of the attack, the computer was just completing a final analysis which would have put the figure so close to 100% that the difference would have been meaningless. A paradise! Hanging there in space, its beauty had so impressed him that he had named it Kensho after one of the stages of Enlightenment. But now 80% of the expedition's personnel—Pilgrims, crew and officers—were dead. And the survivors couldn't stay and couldn't leave. Since they couldn't do either, they'd have to do both. Or neither.

Well, he thought, since neither Aristotilian Logic nor the disciplines of Science seemed to offer much hope, it's time to go beyond them.

He stood, turned the holo-viewer off, and walked slowly over to his meditation spot. On the wall was a scroll bearing his favorite koan, brushworked by a 13th Century Japanese master. Directly in front were zafu and zabuton in black. He knelt, bowed, and then arranged himself on the pillows. Drawing a few deep even breaths, he entered a mental state practiced only by Masters of the Universal Way of Zen. In it his mind floated freely, able to rummage at will among the bits and pieces of data he had absorbed, undistracted by any outside disturbances. Logical structures no longer inhibited him. Pre-conceptions, prejudices, ordinary human standards vanished. All things, those previously trivial as well as those once thought important, became absolutely equal by acquiring an absolute value, revealing relationships not evident to ordinary vision. Like beads strung on a string of their own meaning, each thing pointed to its own common ground of existence, shared by all. Finally, each began to melt into each, staying itself while becoming all others. And Mind no longer contemplated Problem, but became Problem, destroying Subject-Object by becoming them.

Time passed, unheeded.

Eventually, there was a tentative stirring, then a decisive one, and Nakamura arose, a smile on his face and the light of laughter in his eyes.

He had a plan, one that delighted him. It took advantage of all the important aspects of the situation, even the apparently negative ones, and used them all to positive effect. It was as natural as a river finding its way to the sea. Once set in motion, it would proceed as inevitably as a ball rolling down an inclined plane.

Initiating it, however, called for rather harsh sacrifices. His own death was least among these. And he feared that the fate in store for most of his officers, who otherwise would have returned to Earth, was even worse. As for what the Pilgrims would suffer . . . well, only the end results—and the lack of alternative—could justify such means.

Calmly, his back straight and proud, almost as if walking in a ceremonial procession, he approached a small chest against one wall. He knelt before it and bowed his respect. Then he lifted the lid and took out two long bundles wrapped in silk. Reverently, he folded back the cloth to expose a long, slightly curved, two-handed samurai sword in an inlayed ebony scabbard, and a shorter matching dagger in an identical sheath. He pulled the dagger slowly from its sheath and looked thoughtfully at the glistening blade. It was sharp enough to cut a falling hair. Satisfied with what he saw, he replaced the dagger in the sheath and stuck it in his obi belt on the left side. With great care, he rewrapped the sword. He bowed once more, then stood and walked over to the scroll and cushions. On the floor, about two-thirds of the way to the wall from the cushions, he laid the silk-enfolded bundle.

He paused for a few moments of quiet contemplation, letting his eyes wander about the room. Goodbye, he said silently.

Giving himself a slight shake, he turned and strode briskly to the center of the room. Aloud he commanded, "Enter Passive Mode for 200 of this planet's circuits around its primary. Maintain current position with respect to the planetary surface. All external sensors, both planetary and local are to remain in operation. Continue accumulation and correlation of data. Establish and keep constant contact with the Admiral's launch after it lands on the surface. Re-establish Active Mode in both the launch and Flagship immediately upon contact with any descendent of the crew or passengers."

"Aye, aye, sir," came quiet acknowledgement from the air. "Assuming Passive Mode, mark 10,9,8,7,6,5,4,3,2,1,0." The lights dimmed and a thousand little noises, barely discernible before, ceased, their absence startling in the silence.

Nodding satisfaction, Admiral Nakamura turned and walked toward the lift that would take him to his launch. His face was relaxed and a slight smile played about the corners of his mouth.

And now, he thought, to the end . . . and the beginning.

This, then, is the Koan of Nakamura. Hear it well and commit it to memory. Think on it day and night, for therein lies salvation for Mankind on Kensho, salvation from the Mushin and the Madness.

To be free, a man must follow the Way
that leads to the place where he dwelt
before he was born.

Chapter I

THE PRACTICE YARD fell silent. Sensing a presence behind him, Jerome lowered his sword and turned slowly to face Father Ribaud, the Sword Master. Behind Ribaud, standing nervously at the edge of the yard, was a young Messenger dressed in the black robe of one who served the Grandfathers.

A thrill of anticipation ran shivering up Jerome's spine. A Message from the Grandfather! Perhaps his request for Audience was being answered!

Ribaud nodded somberly. "Yes, it's for you. From the Grandfather."

Jerome tried to read the old man's face for information. "Did he say what it's about?"

The Sword Master suppressed a look of amusement. "The simple way to find out is to go over and ask the lad. He's the Messenger, you know, not I. And from the looks of him, he'd be only too glad to deliver his message and be off." Ribaud gestured towards the Messenger, who was anxiously shifting from foot to foot. "He's nervous as a cat, what with all the Mushin floating around this yard. His mind isn't trained to handle it." He turned to the silently standing students. "Which reminds me that no one told the rest of you to stop training and gawk around like a bunch of Novices. Back to work, the lot of you. Start off with five hundred each; head, chest, and wrist cuts, slowly. Control your breath and calm your mind."

Practice began again, each student reciting the Chant of Calmness as he swung his sword in unison with the others. Ribaud watched for a moment, then motioned to Jerome and walked with him over to where the Messenger stood waiting.

"Messenger—Brother Jerome," Ribaud said, and stepped back out of easy earshot, though Jerome knew he would hear every word. He might be old, but Ribaud was still in possession of all his faculties, including an incredible, cat-like swiftness.

The Messenger licked the sweat from the upper lip and focused distressed eyes on Jerome. With pity, Jerome noticed that he already had the glazed, hunted look of those who dealt with the Grandfather on a regular basis. Eventually his gaze would turn blank and dead. Jerome shuddered inwardly. One paid a fearful price to serve the Grandfather.

"Brother Jerome," the Messenger began, his voice cracking a little. "Grandfather bids me call you to his presence. Father Ribaud is to prepare you for Audience. Come as soon as you are ready. I . . . I . . . uh . . . that is all." Abruptly the black-clad youth turned and fled the practice yard.

A sardonic grin on his face, Ribaud sauntered over to where Jerome stood gazing after the retreating Messenger. "So. Audience it is. Face to face with the Grandfather. And I'm to prepare you. No easy task, that. I assume you haven't changed your mind, that you're still determined to go through with it?" The young man nodded firmly. The Sword Master shook his head and sighed. His tone had been bantering, but his concern was obvious.

While Jerome racked his practice sword and changed from padded practice robe to a regular one, Ribaud carefully outlined the proper procedure for Personal Audience with the Grandfather. From time to time the young man would nod or grunt, but otherwise gave no indication he was listening. Ribaud knew otherwise. Nothing really passed Jerome by. He was incredibly quick and bright.

Even while talking, the old man's mind went back some fifteen years to the day he had found Jerome. The lad had been sitting amid the smoking ruins of the farmstead at Waters Meeting, trying to straighten his dead mother's clothing. Ribaud knew the child had witnessed his father's torture, his mother's rape, and the slaughter of both at the hands of the Ronin who had raided the farm.

It still seemed like a miracle that the boy had escaped the Madness. Those few who survived the Ronin were always mad. Death was usually a kindness. Yet that small boy had not only survived, but had somehow retained his sanity. Oh, true, true, rage and madness lurked deep in his eyes. Yet it was not *the* Madness. It was something deep within him, shackled and hidden away in the dark place at the center of his being, not something brought on by the Mushin. It was a madness and rage he owned and controlled so well even the Mushin could not sniff it out.

The routine details out of the way, Ribaud pondered what else he ought to say. At the least he felt he should give the lad some sort of advice; Audience was not without its peril. Men had been known to break in the presence of the Grandfather. And the Mushin hovered constantly, waiting for just such a break to swoop down and bring the Madness.

Not that I'm really worried about Jerome, he hastened to reassure himself. The lad controls his mind very well. Perhaps better than any other Son in the Brotherhood. At times he felt the young man's control was perhaps a little too rigid, too brittle, but there was no question it was effective.

Still, the Sword Master felt a vague, gnawing worry over the idea of Jerome facing the Grandfather. What the young man was asking for had clearly been forbidden by the Grandfather himself. The request could only meet with a refusal. And how would Jerome respond to this inevitable, final denial of his long-cherished dream? Ribaud honestly didn't know, but the possibilities disturbed him. He decided he had to make one last effort to dissuade the lad. There was still time to avoid the danger of Audience.

"Now, my Son, listen as you've never listened before." Jerome looked up, surprised by the Sword Master's sudden urgency.

"This isn't some Brother you're about to face, Jerome. It isn't even a Father. You're up against something you can't deal with the way you would another human being. You can't argue, or bluff, or threaten. No amount of wheedling or cajoling will work. Even logic won't have any effect.

"No, this is beyond your experience, my Son. You're about to face a Grandfather. Think what that means! The Grandfathers saved Mankind from the Madness. They gave us the Way of Passivity to protect us from the Mushin. Directly or indirectly, they rule the lives of every man, woman, and child on Kensho. They're our saviours and our leaders.

"But even after seven generations, they remain a complete mystery to us. We don't know where they came from. There was certainly no sign of them here when we arrived. We still don't understand the nature of their existence or the scope and limit of their powers. And most important, we can't comprehend their motivations. Why did they, an alien race, save us?" The Sword Master shook his head in wonderment.

Jerome smiled. "I'm not afraid of the Grandfathers, even if they are aliens. I don't pretend to understand their motivations, but I really see no reason to quail in their presence just because they look a little odd. No, Father, I have my fear, and my mind, under better control than that."

Ribaud looked grim. "There's more to it than that, young man. There's something about being in the presence of a Grandfather which goes beyond your fear and your control. You've seen what happens to those who serve the Grandfathers, the Messengers. Look into their eyes before you scoff at the danger of being near a Grandfather."

"But I'm only going to be there long enough to ask my question and get his answer," the young man protested. "I'm not going to don the black robes."

"Ah, now we're getting to the crux of it all! Your question. It isn't merely that you are going into the presence of the Grandfather, Jerome. The real problem lies in the reason why you're going."

The young man shook his head wearily. "We've discussed this before, Father. Over and over, we've talked this out. And we always come to the same point."

"But can't you see that what you are doing is challenging the Grandfathers? They've very specifically decreed that the Way of Passivity is the only Way for men on Kensho. Any other Way is too dangerous, too active, too open to Desire and the inevitable chain that leads to Madness."

"But, Father," Jerome interrupted, "the Way of the Sword . . ."

"The Way of the Sword especially has been forbidden," the old man overrode his protest. "After that experience with the Old Master, the decision of the Grandfathers was very clear: No man may walk the Way of the Sword.''

"That was thirty years ago! And besides, you were there. What was so horrible about what happened up on the Mountain? Nothing!''

"You call three Brothers struck down by the Madness nothing?''

"That could have happened right here in the Brotherhood! The Mushin attack wherever they find weakness. Those Brothers were weak.''

"One of those 'weaklings' was my best friend,'' the Sword Master smiled bleakly. "But no, you're right, nothing horrible happened that couldn't have happened right here. I admit that I still remember the experience with fondness.

"But that isn't the point. The point is that the Grandfathers saw danger in the experience. And with their greater understanding and wisdom, in their role as guardians of the human race, they decided that the Way of the Sword was too dangerous. That decree has never been questioned or defied. Until now.''

"I'm not defying,'' Jerome protested. "I'm simply asking the Grandfather to reconsider a ruling that was made long before I was even born. It isn't a question of the whole human race abandoning the Way of Passivity for something untried. The issue is simply whether or not one insignificant Brother can try something different from what the rest of Mankind has been doing for the last 200 years.''

Ribaud looked Jerome straight in the eyes. "No. It is not that simple. By this action you're challenging the authority of the Grandfathers, questioning the rightness of their decisions as leaders of our race. You're calling into the doubt the experience of seven generations of Mankind striving to follow the Way of Passivity and fend off the Mushin. And perhaps worst of all, you're denying and rejecting the words and wisdom of Nakamura. The Way of Passivity *is* the Way alluded to in Nakamura's Koan. It *has* saved us from the Mushin and the Madness.''

The young man's face was hard with determination and resolution as he replied to the Sword Master's accusations. "Nakamura's Koan promises Mankind 'freedom,' not 'safety.' But we're not free, even if we are safe. Who's to say that the Way referred to in the Koan is the Way of Passivity? You? Me? The Grandfathers? Only Nakamura himself knew for sure, and he died before the Grandfathers appeared and brought the Way with them, so he never had a chance to state his feelings one way or the other. I know, I know,'' he hurried on, forestalling Ribaud's objection, "the Grandfathers claim they got the idea for the Way from Nakamura's mind as he lay dying. I know they say it's based on his profound knowledge of the Universal Way of Zen, tailored to meet Mankind's needs here on Kensho. Believe me, I fully appreciate the reasons everyone assumes the Way of Passivity is identical with the Way mentioned in the Koan. But still, it's only an assumption. Only Nakamura could confirm it.''

In a more conciliatory tone he continued. "Father, don't misunderstand me. I don't question that the Way was probably the best defense that could be organized at the time. We're indebted to the Grandfathers for showing us the Way.

"But is defense enough? For seven generations we've defended ourselves. We've never struck back. How can we? We know nothing about the enemy. Only what the Grandfathers tell us, which is virtually nothing.

"And what have seven generations of following the Way of Passivity gained us? A degree of safety and peace. Or better yet, safety and stagnation."

The older man opened his mouth to protest, but Jerome hurried on.

"Yes, stagnation! Look, Father, how many new Brotherhoods and Sisterhoods have been built in your lifetime? How many new farmsteads have been founded? None! Not one. In fact, some, like ours at Waters Meeting, aren't even occupied any longer." A look of remembered pain flicked momentarily in the black depths of Jerome's eyes, like the barely visible tail of a fish at the bottom of a pond. Just the barest movement. Then it was gone, instantly slammed behind the iron wall of his control.

"It's as if . . . as if . . ." For a moment the young man groped for an idea just at the edge of understanding. Finding it, he rushed in pursuit. "Yes! It's as if we've reached some optimum level, some point the Grandfathers don't want us to pass. We're like cattle, penned up in the Brotherhoods or on the farmsteads, completely domesticated and unable to roam the surface of the planet we came to colonize; unable to grow. Instead, we're kept safe and stagnant, cowering under the watchful eyes of the Grandfathers, controlled by the Way of Passivity, defending ourselves against an enemy we can't see and don't understand.

"Father, when the path you're on leads nowhere, you must seek a new path. The Way of Passivity gives us survival—but it leads nowhere. We must find a *new* way, a way to fight back, to strike out at the things which keep us hiding like frightened cattle in the safe little pens the Grandfathers have built for us.

"I don't know the answer. I don't know what the path should be. But I feel the Way of the Sword may have something to offer, something the Way of Passivity is lacking. I don't know. Unless I have a chance to follow the Way of the Sword I never will know. All I ask is that chance."

Ribaud shook his head with weary sadness. "Jerome, my Son, at times wanting must give way to acceptance." Jerome made to reply but the Sword Master held up his hand. "The Way of the Sword, followed to the end, leads to the Madness. Look at the Ronin, boy, look at the mad animals that slaughtered your family. Didn't they carry swords?

"Jerome, the Grandfathers are right, even though you are too young to see it. All young men have strong emotions. And you have reasons to harbor the strongest of all: hate. You control it well; indeed, far beyond what one has a right to expect in one so young. But you have boundless energy and boundless ambition. The Brotherhood is hard on you. It is a life for softer men. But there is no other way for humanity here on Kensho. The Madness lies in wait on any other path.''

Even as he uttered the words, Ribaud felt their utter futility. The lad would not listen, indeed could not listen without doing violence to his own character. And the Grandfather would never allow him to leave the Brotherhood to follow the Way of the Sword. Even though there was truth to what Jerome said, the results of the coming Audience could only be tragic.

Jerome looked down and dug at the dust with his toes. "I know," he began in a normal voice. Then, dropping to a hoarse whisper he continued, "But it means so much to me, Father, so much."

The Sword Master suddenly realized that he was beyond his depth, that he was now treading into the dark recesses of Jerome's desire and need.

Dangerous, he thought, to stir up such ghosts and specters in one who goes to Audience.

Ribaud shook his head. It was time to stop, to calm, to support, to say something, anything, that might help. So little I can say that has any meaning. He felt the leaden weight of his inability to offer anything but platitudes. In truth he knew nothing of the complex creature that stood before him. Nothing but the surface. All he could do was to speak to that surface.

Ribaud shrugged his shoulders in defeat. "Go," he quietly commanded Jerome. "Go to the Grandfather and listen to what he doesn't say as carefully as to what he says. He may speak in what sounds to you like riddles. He may not speak at all. If the first, look for meaning beyond words. If the second, listen to the eloquence of the silence. I can offer nothing more.''

Bowing low, Jerome turned and left the practice yard.

Chapter II

JEROME WALKED SLOWLY toward the Grand-father's cell. The sincerity of Ribaud's concern had affected him more deeply than he liked to admit. He'd never really considered the potential danger that lay in a confrontation with the Grandfather. If the possibility of a refusal had ever entered his mind, he had rejected it long ago, convinced by the very depth of his need that permission would be granted automatically. Audience had simply been something he would have to endure to realize his dream of following the Way of the Sword. And besides, the whole thing had always seemed so far in the future.

Now it was here, however, and the realization that in a few moments he would be face to face with the alien being that ruled the Brotherhood filled him with a vague dread. He thought of the fearful, confused eyes of the Novice Messenger who had summoned him, and of the blank, dead-eyed gaze of the black-clad adults who served the Grandfather, and he shivered.

Get hold of yourself! he commanded silently. To distract himself and gain control over his fear, he began to review everything he knew about the Grandfather. Perhaps, he thought, I might even remember something useful for the coming interview.

The Grandfather dwelt at the very center of the Brotherhood in a small, windowless building that had a single, low door, facing south. The door was crudely made of planks from the Ko tree. Inside, the single room was bare except for a mat, woven from the bark of the same tree, rectangular, beginning at the back wall of the room and ending just short of the door. Sitting on the mat, a little over halfway to the wall, was the Grandfather.

He had seen the Grandfather only once, on the day he had been dedicated to the Brotherhood as a Novice. Since he was an orphan, rather than a Called One, he had been required to present himself to the alien for approval. He could remember little but the creature's huge, glowing, multi-faceted eyes. The rest was mainly a memory of shadow, vague bulk, and an occasional sharp angle. By rumor, of course, he knew a great deal more. The angles had been the Grandfather's stick-like arms and legs: the legs folded in front; the arms, elbows out, resting on the knees. Bulk was the large barrel chest, covered with a hard, chitinous substance rather like the armor the Brothers sometimes wore during sword practice. The head was long and narrow, domed at top and coming to a point at the bottom. Large eyes bisected it. Overall, the effect was of a large, benevolent cockroach; a cockroach that talked, and meditated, and ruled a community of seventy humans, but never, never left his cell.

For Jerome knew that once a Grandfather founded a Brotherhood or a Sisterhood, once the cell at its center had been built, the creature was carried within by his black-clad servants and never came out again. He simply stayed there, sitting, never eating, never even moving as far as anyone could tell. Occasionally he would say something in his high, whispery voice. Then one of his empty-eyed Messengers hastened to do his bidding.

Yet despite this immobility the Grandfather was the heart and soul of the Brotherhood. All important decisions were referred to him, even though he often failed to reply to a question. As often as not, even when he did reply his utterances were unintelligible; nevertheless, even the most incoherent reply was carefully taken down and religiously studied by the Fathers until it inspired a decision.

Coming around the end of the Meditation Hall, which lay just to the south of the Grandfather's cell, Jerome stopped for a moment to gaze across the Emptiness at the tiny building which housed the alien. The lifeless, hardpacked soil of the Emptiness shimmered whitely in the sunlight. Every morning and every evening it was carefully scoured by the Novice Messengers and any living thing, animal or vegetable, was removed and destroyed.

A Messenger, probably the same one, stood by the door, his face averted in respect. As Jerome approached, the lad pulled back the door, letting a splash of light drop into the darkness of the room. Stooping, Jerome entered. The door swung shut and night fell.

For a few moments he stood still, his back to the door. Silently he repeated the Litany of Passivity to calm his thumping heart: *Moons, moons, shining down on waters, moving slowly, moons moving slowly, yet being still. Still the waters, still the moons. Movement, strife, all longing is but a reflection, passing to stillness when the mind is calmed.* He droned through it three times while his eyes adjusted to the dark and he gained enough presence of mind to sit down on his end of the Ko mat.

He sat, legs crossed, hands on his knees, eyes cast down about five feet in front of himself, seeing-but-not-seeing. He regulated his breath. And waited.

And waited.

An incalulable age later there came a rising whisper, a breeze of meaning that gently blew toward him across the dark. "Why this subsection of unity now in this place, interrogation."

Jerome, lulled by the long wait, snapped his mind back into focus. "This subsection of unity has a request," he whispered back.

"Make request apparent to this vessel of totality," came the softly hissing answer.

"This subsection of unity wishes to go to the Old Master on the Mountain to follow the Way of the Sword."

Emotion surged up, threatening to overwhelm the controls Jerome had spent so many years constructing. The Sword! How much it meant to him! As a child he had never even thought of the Sword, never even seen one, for that matter. He was a farmer's son, wed to the land.

But then the Sword had come unbidden into his life, shattering and smashing it into dead, lifeless, bloodsoaked fragments. The Sword of Death, brought by the three Ronin, flashing up, flashing down, cutting, gutting. Three Ronin, men who did not fear the Madness, but who actively sought it out, who invited the Mushin to take over their minds, who reveled in rapine, slaughter, insanity. Three Ronin, three Swords, slashing his life to ribbons, bringing death, death, death.

What demons the Sword had raised only the Sword could lay to rest. Only the Sword of Life could give back what the Sword of Death had taken. The Sword giveth and the Sword taketh away. So be it. Even at seven years of age he had realized that. He had known it deeply, organically, without logic, without words, without even thought. Only by mastering what had destroyed his life could he hope to recreate his life. The Sword had started him on this road. Only by the Sword could he reach his destined end. And somewhere, someway, he would meet the Three and complete the cycle of Death and Life, Life and Death.

When he had come to the Brotherhood, he had thrown himself into his studies with an intensity that had at once gratified and worried the Fathers. In exhaustion he had found release from the demonic visions and memories which constantly lurked in the shadows at the edge of his conscious mind. In the Spiritual Exercises and the Physical Disciplines he had found a way to build an iron wall of control around the turbulent passions and fears that dwelt in the dark center of his being.

Relentlessly he had worked and prepared until as a Sixth Level Son he had been allowed to enter the Way of the Sword with Father Ribaud. Once on the Way, he had redoubled his efforts. With cold fury he practiced each cut, each block, each move, each form until exhaustion felled him. After a short rest, he came back for more. In five years he had learned everything Father Ribaud had to teach. Jerome's technique was flawless, his form polished like glasswood. A perfect machine, all he lacked was the soul, the True Understanding of the Way of the Sword as opposed to the Technique of the Sword. Ribaud had tried to show Jerome the Way. But Ribaud himself was but the Sword Master of an out-of-the-way Brotherhood. He was not a True Master of the Way, not an Enlightened One. He could point out the Path, but since he had never trodden it himself he could not lead Jerome on the Way; he could only indicate the general direction in which it lay. Ribaud, who knew his own limitations, made no bones about it. Jerome knew that there could be no further progress toward his goal unless he found a True Master to study with.

There was such a Master on the Mountain. Known only as the Old Master, he lived in a tiny hut, far up the slopes of the towering Mountain. Years ago, when the Old Master had first appeared in the region, he had singlehandedly wiped out a band of eight Ronin which the Brotherhood had been unable to kill or drive away. Then he settled on the slopes of the Mountain. At first, he had grudgingly accepted a few students from the Brotherhood. As a Fifth Level Son, the young Ribaud had been among them. On the Mountain he had caught just a glimpse of the Real Way, a single Satori experience. He still spoke of the experience with reverence and awe.

Immediately after Ribaud's Satori the Grandfather had handed down a decision. Very clear, very precise: no one was to study the Way of the Sword with the Old Master on the Mountain. The Way of the Sword was too active, too dangerous to Passivity. The sword itself was but a training vehicle, a way-station on the path to Passivity and a technique to fend off the Ronin. Nothing more.

That was thirty years ago. Since then hardly anyone had seen the Old Master. But from time to time the Brotherhood's patrols found the bodies of groups of Ronin, so it was assumed the old man was still alive. Yet the fact remained that for thirty years no one had ascended the Mountain to study the Way of the Sword.

But Jerome knew he had to try. It was the only

way, his only hope! The Grandfather must allow him to go, must not stand in the way of his destiny!

But calm! He must remain calm! To draw down Mushin in the very presence of the Grandfather! Even a Novice wouldn't do anything so foolish, so indicative of a lack of control and a straying from the Way of Passivity. "Moons, moons, shining down . . ." he chanted silently, forcing down the emotions, the hopes, forcing his entire being back down, into a tiny, windowless cell at the center of his soul.

Silence.

And waiting.

Then, eventually, the darkness began to vibrate again. Muffled meaning softly filtered through the black of the cell to his straining ears. It was a chant. One he had never heard before:

The Sword is the Mind.
When the Mind is right, the Sword is right.
When the Mind is not right, the Sword
    is not right.
He who would study the Way of the Sword
    must first study his Mind.

Again and again the Grandfather repeated the chant, his hissing rising and falling. At times his voice seemed to fill the cell, pushing back the darkness. At other times it shrank to a tiny spark, almost overwhelmed by the endless night around them. The chant wound its way into Jerome's mind, down into his soul, curling, twisting like a tiny snake of smoke coming from a fire one had thought was extinguished. Slowly it filled his whole being, until it seemed there was no more room for him inside himself.

Control! Control! He had to regain control! Raised from childhood to fear the Mushin, Jerome was terrified at the very thought of anyone or anything tampering with the carefully constructed fabric of his mind's defenses. For generations, loss of control had meant the Mushin gained control, bringing the Madness that had so nearly destroyed the human race on Kensho.

Now Jerome fought back desperately, instinctively. He closed down his mind. Slowly, agonizingly slowly, he retreated back into the hard, dark core of his being. He shut out the curling chant with its meaning beyond words, he fought to re-integrate himself as a separate entity, to cut himself off from external influence.

Panting, sweating harder than he ever had in the practice yard, Jerome gradually brought himself under control again. Deep within him a huge rage burned, shielded from the Mushin by the black walls of his being. But it burned fiercely all the same.

The Grandfather! The alien had done this to him! Had tried to take over his mind! The Grandfather could do things to his mind! It could do things like the Mushin could do!

Anger, confusion, rage, fear, all contained, all held deep within, fused together in a sudden intuitive leap. The Grandfather and the Mushin! Somehow they were linked, related! The race's benefactor and its worst enemy were somehow tied together!

Revulsion and disgust rose up and twisted into

hatred, joining the other emotions that raged within him. For an instant blind fury and hate spewed across Jerome's mind like a leaping wall of brilliant flame. The explosion was incredible. In one motion he stood and took a single step toward the Grandfather. Almost swifter than thought his hand rose and fell in a lightning arc, striking at the base of the alien's neck.

With a sharp snap the head flew off and smashed against the wall of the cell.

The entire universe stood still. Frozen, his mouth agape, Jerome stood, looking at the crumpled, broken head that lay at the base of the wall. His emotions, his incredible raging fury, were gone, sucked into the cold void of eternity.

Then, in the next instant, the frozen, fragile universe shattered like thin crystal and crashed down upon his head. His mind a blank, Jerome tottered and crumpled to the floor.

Chapter III

CONSCIOUSNESS RETURNED SLOWLY, like an old man dragging himself up a steep flight of stairs. For a while Jerome simply lay there, enjoying the solidity of the floor and the texture of the Ko mat against his cheek. Then memory began to seep through the hazy curtains of his confusion. His hand crept softly across his face to brush away the last fogginess and his eyes opened.

Jerome sat up and looked at the Grandfather. The alien body still sat at the other end of the Ko mat. Over by the wall lay its shattered head.

Memory changed from a seeping trickle to a sweeping flood. Jerome braced himself against it and the first wave broke harmlessly against the walls of his control. Gradually he allowed memory to percolate down through the layers of his mind. As it sank to the core of his being a thought rose to meet and pass it by on the way to consciousness. "I have killed a Grandfather," he whispered. "I have killed a Grandfather."

Hearing the sound of his own voice gave the thought a solidity that made it possible for him to grasp and work with it. Carefully he wove it into the framework of thought through which he interpreted the world.

The Way of Passivity taught that Being caused Desiring. Desiring gave rise to Action. Inevitably, Action led to Frustration. And because of the Mushin, Frustration ended in the Madness. The Way was an attempt to cut off this inevitable sequence by practicing Non-action, or Passivity. The Spiritual exercises and Physical Disciplines of the Way taught the control necessary to rein in Desire, to enclose it behind an iron wall of rigid Passivity. Action based on personal Desire must be avoided. For one Action always engendered another. And that, in turn, brought on another. No single Action could ever satisfy Desire once it ruled a man, and so the chain of Desire and Action would lead to Frustration and eventually to the Madness.

Jerome had fallen into just such a sequence when he allowed himself to be ruled by the personal desire to follow the Way of the Sword. His Desire had forced him to the Action of requesting an Audience. And the Audience had led to the Action of killing the Grandfather.

Now more Action was required. Never had he understood the Way of Passivity more clearly. He had acted, and now he must act again. In doing so he was that much closer to the Madness.

But he had to act; he could no longer stay at the Brotherhood. He didn't know what the Fathers would do when they discovered his crime, but his Desire for life made him unwilling to find out. The Fathers didn't exactly worship the Grandfather, but they did revere and obey the alien. Even Father Ribaud looked upon the Grandfathers as Mankind's saviours from the Mushin and the Madness. There could be little doubt that the Fathers would be shocked by what he had done. How shocked, how angered, he could not guess. But it was perfectly possible that in their anger they might lose control and leave an opening for the Mushin to come pouring in.

Jerome shuddered inwardly. All the Fathers were Masters of at least one of the Ways: Fist, the Staff, or the Sword; all were deadly. He had no wish to face even one of them possessed by the Madness.

Now he must act again. He must leave the Brotherhood. Every thought, every motion, must be geared to the satisfaction of his Desire to leave the Brotherhood. One error, one misstep, and he faced Death.

.So. First he had to figure the lay of the land. He listened for some hint of what was happening in the world outside the dark cell. Quiet. Everything was quiet—which meant no one knew! Surely if any of the Brothers knew he had killed the Grandfather they would be there to take him into custody! So no one knew. Yet.

What was more, there didn't seem to be any

Mushin about. He felt with his mind, searching for the telltale tingling sensation they made at the edge of the mind. Again he felt a sense of surprise. Somehow his killing rage had gone undetected by the Mushin as well!

This was food for thought. It was easy to understand how his act had escaped the notice of the Fathers; the Grandfather had no regular attendants, except for the Messengers who came when they were called. Hence there had been no Fathers in the area when the killing had occurred. In addition, he had been swift and silent. But the Mushin, how had his rage escaped the Mushin? Had his sudden collapse after the blow somehow saved him? Could a *killing* go undetected by the Mushin?

The Mushin! Icy recollection ran like a swift chill up his spine. Just before he had risen to strike he had seen some kind of a link between the Mushin and the Grandfather. On the face of it, the idea seemed absurd. How could the benefactors of Mankind be linked with its enemies?

And yet . . . and yet . . . there could be no mistaking what the Grandfather had been trying to do. Jerome knew because he had experienced it. The Grandfather had been trying to break down his control, to take over his mind. If the alien had succeeded, Jerome would have been helpless to fend off the Mushin, helpless in the face of the Madness.

Thought followed thought to the place where doubts dwelt. Just what were the Grandfathers? Where had they come from? Why had they saved Mankind from the Mushin? What was in it for them? These were questions all men asked themselves but seldom spoke aloud. Mankind's debt to the Grandfathers was too great to allow room for much questioning.

Jerome shook his mind free of the circling doubts. Now was no time for speculation. He had to act. The mystery of the motivations of the Grandfathers and their possible link with the Mushin would have to wait.

He looked at the shape sitting headless at the other end of the Ko mat. The alien had done something to his mind. He couldn't repress a slight shiver.

The thing was dead now, though. It could no longer hurt him. Curiosity grew stronger than fear. No one had ever had such a chance to examine a Grandfather before. He found himself rising and stepping over to examine the upright body.

A shock ran through him.

He stood looking down into an empty husk!

The body was hollow!

There was nothing. No vital organs, no blood, no flesh. Nothing! Dazed, he turned to the wall. A step brought him to the shattered head. He stopped to pick it up: it too was empty. A brittle, empty shell.

So the Grandfathers, like the Mushin, were non-physical, their insect-like shells a mere masquerade. *Like* the Mushin? Perhaps the relationship was closer, much closer!

Battered, reeling from shock after shock, Jerome's mind was pushed over the edge, out into space, out where there was no place to stand and fight, out where his iron control meant nothing. He felt his reality blasted by the winds of Reality. He had either to fall eternally into chaos and Madness or find his wings and fly.

He became unsane. He passed the boundaries of Self and looked back at the pathetic creature which stood in a dark cell and held the crumpled head of a Grandfather in its hand. He saw himself with complete objectivity, as he really was. He saw the hollowness of the alien's shell. And the hollowness of his own.

His shell. His armor. The beloved wall of control he had so carefully and lavishly constructed. It did not enclose some lovely garden, some orderly place that had to be protected against the dangers of the outside world. Within those iron walls there was no Calm, no Passivity, nothing to mirror or match the rigid exterior. There was only a vast, foul, seething void of incoherent passion and Desire, a cesspool of terror held back by the weakest of restraints.

He knew this was the Truth. The Passivity was shallow, a brittle shell, a lie that gave a smiling face to a snarling beast. It did not go the core. It simply contained it.

Like a visiting specter, he floated through the agony that filled his Center. He heard again the bellows of his father, writhing in his bonds as three Ronin raped and murdered his mother. Once more he pulled his parents' bodies from the burning house. His fear of the older Sons was there too, as were the fights behind the Refectory, and the drubbings he had had to endure in silence.

All the anguish of his life was there. All compressed, all repressed behind the control the Passivity taught.

He knew this was the Truth. The Passivity did not do what the Grandfathers claimed. It did not set the men free from Desire. Desire was still there, made more intense than ever by being subverted and hidden. The Passivity did not do away with the Frustration caused by Action: it merely changed the nature of the Frustration and locked it behind the iron control of the Spiritual Exercises and Physical Disciplines.

He knew this was the Truth, and the Light of it shone brightly on his soul. So bright was the Light that he could see the Way he must follow. A brief, dim glimpse, but a seeing none the less.

The Center must be Calm. The Way of the Passivity did not accomplish this. His Way lay up the path to the clearing on the Mountain where the Old Master sat, waiting. There he would study the Way of the Sword. There he would strive to calm his Center so that the walls of control were no longer necessary. There he would seek the Way of Nakamura's Koan, the Way to set all Mankind on Kensho free of the Mushin and the Madness and the Grandfathers. The Light did not show him the end of the Way he must follow. But it showed him the beginning. It was enough.

Gradually the Light dimmed and he became Brother Jerome, standing in a dark cell with the crumpled head of a Grandfather in his hand. Carefully, almost gently, he placed the head back on the floor, turned and walked softly to the door of the cell.

Now he had to tune his every sense to escape.

He no longer feared Action, nor Frustration, nor the Madness. Action was necessary to the following of his Way. He peered out one of the cracks between the planks. He saw nothing. Startled, he realized it was dark. Which meant he must have been sitting with the Grandfather for hours! He pressed his ear to the door, listening for outside activity, for the sound of the bell in the Meditation Hall, for the clash of dishes from the Refectory, for anything that could give him a clue as to what was happening outside.

Nothing. The world was still.

That could only mean it was late at night, long after all the Novices, Sons, and Fathers had finished Evening Sitting and gone to their cells for Final Meditation and Rest. In other words, the Brotherhood was asleep. There were Novices guarding the North and South Ways, of course, but Jerome could avoid them and go over the wall.

Carefully planning his every move, Jerome reviewed the layout of the Brotherhood. On the north, east, and west of the Grandfather's cell, well beyond the Emptiness, were the long, low buildings which housed the Fathers. On the north, east, and west of the Grandfather's cell, well beyond the Emptiness, were the long, low buildings which housed the Fathers. Further to the east was the practice yard for the Soft Way, to the west the yard for the Staff, and on the north the classrooms and several workshops. Best not to pass that way. Too many people. Best to go south. There lay the Meditation Hall, a roof supported by pillars. He would see no one there this time of night. Once

past the Hall, he would have to pass the Foundry
and the Smithy, busy spots during the day as the
Fathers manufactured the metal tools and implements the Brotherhood was famous for. But now
all would lie silent and empty. Beyond these two
buildings squatted the form of the Refectory with
its long tables and hot, steamy kitchens. To the
east, in the angle made by the wall around the
Brotherhood, was the practice yard for the Fist. At
the northern end of this yard, built into the very
wall, was his tiny cell.

Yes, he thought, yes, that's the way to go. Every
step of the way was clear in his mind. Time for
Action, he decided. Slowly he opened the door
outward, its squeak startling him with its loudness.
Cautiously he looked around, then stepped out
and gently closed the door behind him, wincing at
the sound. No one heard. The world remained
silent.

A breeze blew across his face, making him suddenly aware he was sweating. He grimaced. I'm
afraid, he thought. Scared. Walking softly as he
had been trained by the Fist Master, Jerome
crossed the Emptiness. He moved south, around
the Meditation Hall, hollow and cold in the light of
two of Kensho's four moons. He passed quickly by
the empty darkness of the Smithy, then turned
sharply to the east, just skirting the north end of
the practice yard.

The breeze blew steadily, cooling his forehead
and chasing through his hair. All around him the
silence kept watch. Once he heard the ting-ting of
the North Way Watch sounding the hour and the

South Way Watch responding. It was the second hour. He had been with the Grandfather for at least twelve hours!

At the door of his cell he stopped. Why had he come back here? There was nothing within worth this dangerous delay. Only his bowl, his knife, a spare robe and his Smoothstone. Oh, yes, and an old, worn pair of sandals.

One more thing, too. One more thing. Something he never admitted he had, never showed to anyone, almost never looked at himself. It was under the straw pallet. He reached under the thin mattress and groped for it.

When his fingers closed over its cool hardness, he drew it forth. It was a small badge, attached to a crudely made chain. His mother had worn it around her neck. He had taken it from her dead body as he sat mourning amid the smoke and stink of the farmstead at Waters Meeting. It was his father's actually, something that had been handed down from father to son ever since the Early days. Had it not been for the Ronin, one day Jerome's wife would have worn it. Jerome held it up in the beam of moonslight that filtered into his cell from the ventilation slit in the ceiling. He could just make out the words inscribed on the dull surface: "P. Rausch Chief Engineer." He slipped the chain over his head and hid the badge beneath the coarse cloth of his robe.

Moving swiftly now, anxious to leave, he placed the sandals, bowl, Smoothstone, knife, and a pair of eating sticks on the spare robe. He folded the bottom up and rolled the whole thing into a tight knot to secure the loose items. A string around the middle assured it wouldn't come apart. Finally he looped the whole thing around one shoulder and across his waist and tied the sleeves in front.

Once outside again, he turned south around the Smithy to keep as many buildings as possible between himself and the dwellings of the Fathers. The Foundry was soon passed on his right and he found himself at the north end of the practice yard where the Sword was taught. For a moment he paused, then he moved south and entered the yard itself. He strode swiftly to the rack where the swords were kept. Fondly he took down his favorite, Whistler, held it lovingly.

For a few moments he stood there gazing at it, experiencing the good memories it awakened of hours sweating in the sun perfecting his stroke and cut. Father Ribaud's presence filled the moonslit yard and Jerome felt a lump in his throat. The old man would be stunned by what had happened. Jerome would give anything to see him one last time, to attempt to explain what his revelation had shown, and what path he must now follow. But as much as he loved the Sword Master he realized they could not communicate on certain things, that their views were too widely divergent to make understanding possible. Sympathy, yes. But not understanding.

He must go his own way now. He would take Father Ribaud with him, in his heart, wherever he went. But the journey itself must be made alone.

And the sword, Whistler, should he take it with him? The world he was entering was dangerous and the sword might make the difference between survival and death. He paused only a moment and then returned the sword to the rack.

No, it wasn't right. Not because it would be stealing, but because he knew intuitively that he would have to earn his sword, not just take it. He knew he was increasing his chance of death greatly by not taking the weapon, but that risk was one he had known about when he had decided to walk the Way. Now he was a Seeker of the Way. He would have to find his own sword somewhere on the journey. He bowed to the Shrine of the practice yard and left.

Jerome was now at the west wall of the Brotherhood. Here there were some sheds with sloping roofs that were used for the storage of tools. They offered easy access to the top of the wall. Looking around briefly one last time, Jerome began to climb.

Chapter IV

AN HOUR'S BRISK walk brought Jerome to the crest of the first of a range of small but steep hills which filled the V made by the meeting of the Big and Little Waters. All four of Kensho's moons filled the sky, so it was easy to pick his way. Behind him, the first purple flush of dawn had begun to tint the sky. Reaching the top, he stopped and turned, looking intently back the way he had come.

Satisfied at last that there were no signs of pursuit, he relaxed, but continued looking off toward the sunrise. There, in the distant foreground, was the still-dark bulk of the Brotherhood. Far down the great valley that had been cut by the Waters, so indistinct that no one would have noticed it if he

49

didn't know what to look for, was a brownish-grey smudge that marked what remained of the farmstead at Waters Meeting. As he gazed, he was struck by the thought that this was his own past he saw, laid out beneath the moonlight and the dawn.

Feeling uncomfortable with the past, he tried to dismiss it with a shrug. Unsuccessful, he turned his back on it and looked westward after the fleeing moons and the retreating darkness. Here and there, sometimes in the valleys between the hills, sometimes clinging to their steep sides, dense groves of Firewood trees squatted, isolated from each other, yet giving promise of the forest to come. Further on, the foothills rose and the Wood itself began. Beyond that, he could just make out the dark mass of The Mountain, its dawnlit peak seeming to float in emptiness. The Mountain was the highest peak in the crescent-shaped range that cupped the lands settled by the humans and held them against the vast Sea to the east.

If what lay behind was his past, what he now faced was his future. It was still dark and unknown, but there was the hope of light to come promised by the Mountain. On those unlit slopes were the Master and the Way of the Sword.

Well, he thought, now all I have to do is get there. There were two ways he could travel. The first would be to head northwest, out of the hills, to follow the broad valley of the Big Water. This fertile region was dotted with farmsteads, each surrounded by a sturdy stockade to help protect it from roving bands of Ronin. There were even roads in the valley, maintained by the Brotherhoods and used by them and the Sisterhoods to transport raw materials and finished goods from place to place. It would be an easy, safe way to travel—unless, of course, someone was looking for him, searching for the killer of the Grandfather. Then the word would travel swiftly, more swiftly than he, and the safe way would become a trap.

He frowned. No, that was not the way to go. Better to stick to the hills. The soil was poorer here. So there were fewer farmsteads. No roads, either, except for the narrow tracks that twisted along the valley bottoms.

Of course, though pursuit would be hampered, there was greater danger here of a different kind. Ronin hid in the hills, using the isolation and sparse population to cover their whereabouts and movements. He'd have to go cautiously. Also, since there were fewer farmsteads, he'd find it harder to obtain food and lodging. Some nights he'd be forced to sleep beneath the stars and go to bed hungry. Oh, well, he shrugged to himself, I never expected this to be easy.

The hills it is then, he decided. He moved his shoulders to settle his makeshift pack more comfortably. Without casting a backward glance, he strode off down the hill, picking a landmark on the opposite slope to aim for.

By late afternoon, he was footsore and ravenous with hunger. From the hill where he stood, he could see a thin line of smoke rising into the sunlight. Beyond the next hill, he estimated. In the valley. Even a stale piece of dried Ken-cow would be delicious about now. He'd have to approach the farmstead carefully so as not to frighten the 'steader and his family. Wouldn't do to be mistaken for a Ronin, he reminded himself. They'd feed a Brother, but one they took for a Ronin would meet with the blankness of barred doors and tightly shuttered windows.

Luckily, the 'stead was in an open glade in the bottom of a rather wide valley. He approached slowly, letting the 'steader get a good look at his brown Brotherhood robe. A long distance off, he held up his right hand, palm open and upward, in the signal the Brotherhood used to denote "friend". Give him every assurance, he thought, give him every opportunity to accept you.

About twenty-five paces away, Jerome came to a halt. He pulled the hood of his robe off his head to show himself completely to the man. Then he bowed, from the waist, his arms spread out, palms forward, in the standard greeting of peace.

"I am without Desire and free of Mushin," he called out in the traditional opening.

The 'steader looked stolidly about at the wall of trees edging the glade, looking for the slightest hint of lurking enemies. For several moments he didn't reply. Then he looked at the young Brother and responded, "There are no Mushin here. If you come without Desire, you will find Calm."

The formalities over, Jerome smiled. "I come with an empty belly!" he laughed. "Have you any work so a poor Brother can earn a bite to eat?"

"Ha! Work? I've years of it! I was hoeing the garden when I caught glimpse of you at the edge of the wood. And there's wood to split. And the stockade gate to mend. And . . . Ha! I've enough work to fill up three bellies!'' The 'steader turned to the cabin and called out, ''Maya, bring something for this young man to eat! We'll get no work out of a starvin' man! And Lester, you bring the extra axe. We've help for the wood pile!''

In addition to the Ken-cows and crops raised by every 'steader, here they cut Firewood for a nearby Brotherhood that smelted the iron ore dug out of the hills to the north. As a result, the ''wood pile'' turned out to be a wood mountain. For three hours, the 'steader, his twelve-year-old son, and Jerome worked steadily. Jerome enjoyed the feeling of the swinging axe, the rhythm the work set up in his body. His mind floated free and soft. Detached, simply being in his body, he was happy and relaxed.

As the shadows began to lengthen and darken in the valley, the older man called a halt to the labor. He clapped Jerome on the shoulder. ''You work well, young man. Silent, strong, steady. You'll have a good meal and a place to rest tonight. And if you'll stay another day, you'll have the same. If not, we'll give you a bit to take with you on your way.'' He turned and began to walk toward the cabin. ''Come,'' he gestured over his shoulder. ''Lester, put the axes away, lad. You too have earned a man's meal tonight!''

The cabin was cozy, warmed by the firelight and the people who lived there. The 'steader's wife was a large woman, with skin as smooth as her husband's was rough. Only around the eyes and mouth corners were there wrinkles, and those spoke of smiles rather than frowns. No one asked Jerome his business, the purpose of his journey, or anything personal about himself or his life. They simply accepted him, spoke of the immediate things of the day, and enjoyed each other's existence.

Finally, though, the father looked at the young man and said, "So you're a Brother, then. From a way off, I reckon, since I don't think I've seen you at the Iron Brotherhood. Besides, you came from the southeast, and they're to the north."

He turned and motioned to his son. "Lester here has been Called. We were told of it last time we delivered wood to the Brotherhood. Imagine! Only twelve and Called! A bright boy, our Lester."

For several moments there was silence in the single room. The light from the fire flickered across their faces and bounced about on the shutters which were locked into place across the windows as protection against night-marauding Ronin. The door was also barred. Lester turned from the fire and looked up at Jerome. Visibly awed at first, at last he worked up his courage to ask a question. "What's it like to be a Brother?"

Jerome looked at the boy and felt a sudden ache, an empty feeling which filled his chest. He looked down at the floor. Called at twelve! Lucky!? I was never Called, he thought. I never reached an age where Calling was possible. At seven I was an orphan! That was bad enough. But to leave all this, after twelve years? He found he couldn't even articulate what he felt—jealousy, sorrow, concern, all churned together into an indescribable sense of personal loss. Silently, he started the Litany to calm his mind. "Moons, moons, shining down on waters, waters. . . ."

Only a moment passed and he looked up again at Lester, his eyes calm and friendly. "What's it like to be a Brother? Ah! It's harder than chopping wood! And easier. You'll find the food's not as good as your mother's!"

The boy shook his head, a slight smile on his lips. "No. No, I don't mean that. I mean what's it like to be somewhere where they are so many Mushin all the time?"

Jerome looked sharply at the quiet, intelligent face of the lad. "What? So many Mushin? Aren't there Mushin around here?"

The 'steader smiled. "Sure. One or two. Now and then. But not like at the Brotherhood! Whew! It's all a body can do to keep his head when you're at that Brotherhood."

"I always feel so many when Dad and I deliver the wood. The closer we come to the Brotherhood, the more there are. And once we're within the walls! Millions of 'em!" He caught his father's look. "Well, maybe hundreds. Is that why they have to study the Way so carefully at the Brotherhoods? Because there are so many Mushin?"

"I . . . I . . . don't quite understand," replied Jerome, confusion clear on his face. "Are you saying that there aren't any Mushin around here, that they're all at the Brotherhood?"

"Seems like it," shrugged Lester.

"Well, now, it isn't that there aren't any here.

Just aren't so many is all," the 'steader's wife spoke up. " 'Course with all those folks doing all those things in such a small area, bound to be more Mushin there than out here in the woods." She smiled at Jerome. "Only way we can survive without much training in the Way is if there aren't too many Mushin around. That stands to reason."

This was something new to Jerome. More Mushin around a Brotherhood than out here in the woods? He had always assumed that the enemy was pretty evenly spread out, seeking prey wherever and whenever they could find it. Tentatively, he reached out with his mind to search for the telltale tingling sensation that Mushin produced if they were in the area. Nothing! Four people in the same room and not a sign of Mushin! Of course, he realized as he looked around, this seems to be an unusually calm group of people. The way they talk, it almost sounds as if the Mushin don't really bother them.

Not quite knowing what to make of this information, and realizing that he still had not responded to his hosts' questions, Jerome filed it away for later consideration. He'd never lived anywhere but the Brotherhood, so he had no way of knowing if this was common or unusual. But more Mushin around the Brotherhood!? He shook his head in amazement.

Turning to Lester, he said, "Well, yes, the Mushin are the reason we have to study the Way so hard. But then all men and women study the Way. Just in different degrees, that's all. You won't find it hard. After a few years, you'll be able to engage in almost any activity and still be free of the Mushin. Of course you have to be constantly on guard . . ."

"But why?" the boy interrupted. "I'm not on guard here." He looked quizzically at Jerome, as though disappointed with what the young man was saying. "If there are so many Mushin around the Brotherhoods that the Brothers have to concentrate day and night, why don't they just leave and go back to the 'steads they came from?"

Seeing Jerome's discomfiture at the question, the 'steader stepped in. "Well, now, this here is only a Brother, Lester. The lad's not a Father. Surely you can't expect him to know all the answers. Besides, you'll learn first hand soon enough. You'll be going with the new group of Called Ones just after the harvest."

Lester nodded. "I'd rather not, but I guess one can't question the decisions of the Grandfathers. At least not until one knows more."

The 'steader stood to end the discussion. "Time to sleep. Got a lot to do tomorrow. Will you be staying or heading on in the morning, young Brother?"

"Heading on," Jerome replied quietly, his mind still running around the edges of the new information he had acquired.

"Well, good enough, then. Sleep over there by the window. At first light we'll put up some food for you and see you on your way. And thanks to you for chopping so much wood." He chuckled. "And for listening to Lester."

Lying next to the wall beneath the window, Jerome engaged in several hours of restless thinking. Arriving nowhere, he finally stopped and let sleep catch up with him.

The 'steader's wife had been more than generous. Even though Jerome didn't find another farmstead that evening, he had plenty to eat. It was a fine night, so he didn't really mind sleeping out.

The next day wasn't quite as pleasant, however. Dawn was heralded not by the sun, but with a cloudburst that settled down to a steady drizzle as the day wore on. Since movement was the only way to keep warm, Jerome decided to travel despite the weather. That evening it cleared off and he gobbled down the last crumbs of food from the night before. It was a hungry, uncomfortable night.

By now he had reached the foothills and the beginnings of the Wood. To the south, the hills were still relatively open and free of trees. But to the north and west the Wood covered everything, with only The Mountain and some of the other peaks of the range showing above the forest. Traveling here would be harder, slower. The foothills themselves were steep and the tree cover made navigation difficult. His best bet would be to follow a stream that ran down from The Mountain. Traveling in the valley bottom would be easier and he could generally be sure he was heading in the right direction. If he got lost, he'd have to climb a ridge and get to the top of the tallest tree to take his bearings again.

As dawn broke, he gathered a few berries and started on his way. Looking up to take his bearings he noticed something unusual off to the southwest: a column of smoke slashing the dawn like an exclamation point. And there were tiny dots in the sky, spiraling lazily around the column.

For a moment he stared, uncertain. What chimney would make so much smoke? Or was it smoke? Then it hit him. It was smoke, but not from a chimney. And those dots, slowly wheeling in the sky. . . .

He recognized the signs. Once that same sentinel of smoke, those same patient, leathery wings, had hovered like a beacon of doom over his childhood home, the farmstead at Waters Meeting. Vividly he remembered how the Ronin had come screaming out of the night. They had raped and slaughtered his mother, tortured and murdered his father. His sister had died quickly, her brains splattered against the door frame as one of the raiders swung her round and round by her heels. He, a tiny, terrified boy huddling beneath a pile of sacks where his mother had thrust him as the Ronin broke down the cabin door, had watched the whole thing.

And he had survived. That was unusual; the Ronin were viciously thorough, seldom leaving anything alive, man or beast, on any farmstead they attacked. Yet somehow no one had bothered to check the pile of sacks beneath which he cowered.

Later, when the Ronin had put the farmstead to the torch and had gone howling off into the night, he had managed to drag his parents' mutilated bodies from the inferno. The roof and walls collapsed before he could pull out his sister.

The next morning, the Fathers from the nearby Brotherhood had followed the column of smoke and the circling carrion lizards to where the young boy sat, crying, but calmly adjusting his mother's clothing and shooing away the most insistent lizards.

That had been fifteen years ago. But the world had not changed, and Jerome knew what to expect as he, in his turn, followed the smoke and the circling lizards.

He paused for a moment at the smashed, sagging gate of the pathetically inadequate stockade. The Ronin had simply shattered it, using a log as a battering ram. What had not burnt leaned at crazy angles, only waiting for time or a strong wind to send it tumbling.

For a moment longer he stood, calming his mind, steeling himself for what he knew awaited. Regulating his breathing, he silently let the Litany of Passivity roll softly through his mind. "Moons, moons, shining down on waters, waters . . ." As ready as he would ever be, he stepped through the gate and entered the smoking charnel house.

What he found sickened him. There had been five in the family. The boy had been about nine. The two girls perhaps six and two. It was hard to tell; there was little left of them. The Ronin had hacked the bodies into pieces and the fire had disfigured what was left.

He rummaged about the smoldering ruins, keeping tight rein on his revulsion and rage. It took all his training to contain himself, to wrap his seething inner turmoil in a calm exterior. But it was necessary. If any Mushin were still lurking about they would get nothing from him. They had feasted enough last night!

In a sod shed which had not burned, he found a shovel. On a grassy knoll north of the house he dug a shallow pit. Then he went back to the ruin, shooed away the carrion lizards, and stuffed what he could find of the family in a pair of old sacks also discovered in the shed—he didn't bother to sort out the pieces. They wouldn't care anyway. When one sack was full, he filled the other. Both were dragged to the pit, thrown in, and covered with the crumbly grey soil the 'steader had tilled in life.

He paused for a moment over the freshly filled grave. There should be something he could say, some fitting memorial for the massacred family. Some phrase that might exorcise the ghost of memory that arose on seeing in others the fate of his own family.

His mind was blank. Faced with real, palpable death, he could only feel a dull grief for himself, his family, and these nameless, hapless 'steaders. There was nothing he could say about the tragedy. It was too total, too awful, too ordinary.

Yet as he stood there, the dull ache began to fade before a rising glow of rage. The Mushin, he thought. That's where it all lies. The Mushin. The Ronin are nothing but tools, men who enjoy the bloodlust, the Madness, the intensified thrill of killing which the presence of the Mushin gives them. The Ronin live to kill, and the Mushin live off the blazing lust and searing emotions the Ronin feel as they kill. Get rid of the Mushin and the Ronin will quickly fade.

Get rid of the Mushin.

Until Man could escape the Mushin he was doomed to a miserable existence, huddling in constant terror on the farmsteads or hiding in fear behind the skirts of the alien Grandfathers. Until Man found a way to strike back at the invisible enemies that fed off his emotions and brought the Madness, he would stagnate, never growing nor expanding here on Kensho.

Nothing said over this grave will make any difference, he realized. Nothing said anywhere will make any difference. Only what I do can make a difference.

Action. Action against the Mushin. That was the only hope. The Fathers, the Grandfathers, the Brotherhood and the Sisterhood; they were all *wrong*. The Way of Passivity was not enough. There must be action, an active seeking out of ways to fight back. If he succeeded in his quest, if the Way he sought did reveal a way to fight back, then he would be raising a monument, a memorial to this family and to every family that had ever been slaughtered by the Ronin. He would be avenging every human ever driven to the Madness by the Mushin.

Jerome turned from the grave. There was nothing to say. But there was a great deal to do.

Chapter V

FOR THE REST of the morning Jerome followed the tracks of the Ronin. At first he cursed the luck that had put them ahead of him; like him, they were heading up the slopes of the Mountain.

At all costs, he wanted to avoid them. As near as he could tell, there were five or six in the band, an unusually large number. Two or three was more common, for Ronin were as dangerous to each other as they were to other men. When no easier prey was at hand they would fall on each other with the same fierce abandon they practiced on the 'steaders. In larger bands the tensions between the members were greater, and so were the chances of mutual mayhem. No Ronin lived long, but those who ran in small packs lived longer.

In any case, there were at least five of them, all armed with swords. Whereas he was alone, and armed merely with a knife and a wooden staff he had cut at the edge of the Wood. And even if he'd had a sword, one Sixth Level Son, no matter how polished his technique, was no match for half a dozen Mushin-crazed Ronin.

But what was the best way to avoid them? He could climb out of the valley and cut across the ridges, hoping to find another valley up which he could travel, or he might stick to the ridges, though the going would be rough. But in either case, he still might cross their path. As long as they remained above him on the slopes, there was no way he could be sure of avoiding them.

He had finally decided that the wisest course was to stick with the known and follow the Ronin as long as they stayed in this valley. That way he would always know approximately where they were, though he'd have to travel cautiously to avoid closing with them from behind.

As he moved up the valley, all senses alert for any sign of the Ronin, the forest closed in slowly from the ridges until trees filled the valley from rim to rim. Soon his view of the Mountain, shining in the morning sun, was cut off. More important, his view ahead was cut down drastically: he could see barely a few hundred feet ahead into the gloom and undergrowth. The blazes of sunlight that broke through the forest cover here and there only served to emphasize the shadows without greatly improving visibility.

When the sun had climbed to the highest point in

the sky Jerome rested for a while. He drank from a small stream that gently chuckled its way between the trees, and ate the fruit of the ubiquitous and ever-bountiful Ko tree. Soon the gentle warmth of noontime and the quiet solemnity of the forest lulled him into a half-doze.

Suddenly he sat bolt upright straining to hear. All drowsiness vanished in an instant; off in the distance he could barely make out a faint, high-pitched yelping. It was instantly joined by a chorus of other yowlings, mewlings, bellowings—an unholy choir of sub-bestial sounds that could only come from the throats of Mushin-crazed men.

Somewhere up ahead of him the band had run across prey and was giving chase!

Casting all caution to the winds, Jerome ran crashing through the forest in the direction of the howling. Sometimes 'steaders built their cabins in the clearings that dotted the Wood, ignoring danger for the sake of the rich soil to be found there. Perhaps the Ronin had found such a family, and even now were attacking.

As he ran, dodging the major branches, accepting constant swattings from the smaller ones, he calmed his mind. It was foolishness to run headlong into combat with six armed Ronin, but what could he do? His own childhood experience, his recent discovery of the atrocity down the valley—his very sense of humanity—made it impossible to stand calmly by while Ronin massacred another family.

Abruptly Jerome all but tumbled out onto the soft turf carpeting a clearing, and came to a skidding halt. Like a solid wall, the combined presence of hundreds of Mushin struck his mind. Instead of the usual tingling that revealed their presence he felt a virtual burning in his mind.

With frantic haste Jerome closed down his mind, asserting the controls taught him by the Fathers. He began chanting the Litany. ''Moons, moons, shining down on waters, waters, moving slowly, moons moving slowly, yet being still. Still the waters, still the moons. Movement, strife, all longing is but a reflection, passing to stillness when the mind is calmed.''

Looking around he located the Ronin and their prey. The six were in a circle surrounding a lone man. The victim, dressed in a robe of coarse homespun, was old, his hair a shining white blaze in the light that poured into the clearing.

Calmer now, Jerome began to notice other things. The old man had a sword, but it was still sheathed. He stood quietly in the middle of the circling Ronin, silent and unruffled. His head was bowed as though he were concentrating on a bug crawling in the grass at his feet.

Jerome hesitated. The Ronin had not seen him. They were too intent on their prey. And there was no way they could have heard his crashing approach, because their own howlings were so loud they drowned out any other sound. Nor did the Mushin sense his presence, so tight was his control. But what should he do?

Before he had time to decide, the Ronin stopped circling and rushed in to attack their victim. The raider standing directly behind the old man was in the lead, hoping to make the kill from behind, his sword raised, flashing in the light, his mouth open in screaming anticipation of the slaughter.

Without looking to right or left, the old man's head snapped up and at the same instant he drew his weapon. But rather than moving forward, he stepped back and simply slid the sword backward, impaling the charging attacker behind him. In and out the blade flicked, and the howling changed to a choked gurgle as the Ronin collapsed in a heap. As the prey had drawn his sword, those attackers in front had checked their headlong assault, expecting him to come toward them. Now his sword swept around leftward from behind slicing through the ribs of the raider there, just below his upraised arms. The arc continued, flinging blood behind it, across the front, barely missing three madly back-pedaling Ronin, and catching the one on the far right who had failed to anticipate the full extent of the sword's arc. Both his wrists were cut through, his sword, hands still holding it, sailed lazily through the air.

Now the old man's sword turned in mid-air, reversing its sweep, coming down and under, the tip almost touching the grass. The raider on the left, seeing the man on the right fall, had stepped in to strike. He met death as the blade swept under his guard, entering his body at the groin and leaving just under the sternum. The old man stepped back, pulled the flying sword with him, cutting edge uppermost. Stepping forward and to the left, he isolated the far right Ronin behind his companion, allowing him to deal with them one at a time.

As the sword had flicked in, it flicked back out, catching the closest man in the throat. A quick step, a final thrust, and the last of the killers lay gurgling out his life in the clearing.

The old man cleaned his blade with a mighty sweep of his sword, a sweep which spatted blood and flesh in a centrifugal fountain of gore. Then, with a deft movement, he returned it to its scabbard and stood quietly gazing at the huddled bodies surrounding him.

Utterly stunned, Jerome stood rooted to the spot, barely able to breathe. It had all lasted the merest moment, the flicker of an eyelash. While Jerome had been trying to make up his mind, the old man had settled the issue completely and finally.

And what swordsmanship! Never in his fondest dreams had Jerome even imagined such a display. The sword had flown on its way, without pause, without uncertainty, without ever missing its mark! It was as though the blade itself had been alive, seeking and finding the vulnerable spots in its enemies' defenses as surely as the Ko-bee finds the just-opening blossom, as lightly as a fluff-fly fluttering in a beam of moonlight. A sense of awe spread through Jerome.

"You may approach. They are all dead." The old man's voice carried across the clearing the way Father Ribaud's had in the practice yard at the Brotherhood. It was low, calm and strong, pitched just right to be heard clearly and distinctly even at a distance. "Come. Even the Mushin might have left to seek new prey. There is nothing here to feed on. I have no emotions and yours are under tight control. The only thing this pile of carrion will draw now is a flock of lizards."

With a huge shake to loosen his taut muscles, Jerome moved softly across the clearing until he was standing next to the old man. The whole situation held a quality of dream to it, a sense of unreality, of things barely considered, half glimpsed in surprise.

The swordsman sighed hugely. "Help me gather up their swords. It would be wasteful to let them rust away."

Still dazzled, Jerome bent unquestioningly to the task. A thought was slowly rising to consciousness. With it came a sense of excitement almost too intense to bear. He had been on his way up the Mountain to find the fabled Old Master and study the Way of the Sword. What he had just witnessed was without a doubt the most incredible display of swordsmanship ever seen. This old man dressed in homespun, bending down next to him to relieve the dead Ronin of their swords, this man must be the Old Master himself!

Jerome straightened, two sheathed swords in his hands. He held them out to the old man. The white-haired swordsman looked at him quizzically, his own hands full with the other four swords. "Am I to grow two new hands to hold them all?" He laughed lightly. "Keep one yourself, for I see you go unarmed. A dangerous habit in a world where creatures like this," he spurned a fallen raider with a sandaled foot, "wander about at will."

Trembling with the intensity of his excitement, Jerome tried to speak. "I . . . I . . . you must be the Old Master," he blurted out.

The man in the homespun robe cocked his head to one side, a musing smile spreading across his features. "Master? I? You must be mistaken. I'm merely a hermit who lives far up the slope of the Mountain. No Master I, just a hermit."

Jerome stood, befuddled. "But . . . but . . . you must be the Master, the True Master Father Ribaud spoke of. Surely you remember him. He was one of those who came up from the Brotherhood many years ago to study the sword with you."

Laying down the four swords he held and taking the two Jerome offered, the old man shook his head in negation. "Ribaud? No. The name means nothing to me. Perhaps you refer to the hermit who lived in the hut before me. Perhaps he knew this Ribaud."

His confusion growing, Jerome blurted out, "But I've never seen or even dreamt of such swordsmanship! Don't you see? I've left the Brotherhood, come all this way to study the Way of the Sword with you. You must be the Master!"

"I don't 'must' be anything," the other replied sharply. "Least of all a True Master. Or even a plain Master. I've never studied the Sword nor any other Way. Such nonsense is for the Brotherhood, not me." He bent down and tied a cord around the six swords. "Now, if you're not interested in one of these swords, I'll be going back to the peace and quiet of my hut. I've better things to do than stand about chattering with a young fool." With that, he hoisted the bundle of swords on his shoulder, and, stepping over the corpses, headed for the woods at the edge of the clearing.

For a few moments Jerome just stood there, too surprised to move. Then with a curse, he started after the old man, hurrying to catch up. This is the Master, he thought. I know it. But Masters are notoriously hard to deal with and this one has not had a student in many years. But I will not give up. This way lies my path.

Up the Mountain the old man tramped, occasionally looking over his shoulder at Jerome and muttering his irritation. Stolidly, relentlessly, silently, Jerome followed the Master.

The dark of the forest kept him from seeing the glint of secret pleasure and satisfaction that lit the old man's eyes.

Chapter VI

THE LIGHT WAS fading from the sky by the time they reached the Master's hut. The old man went inside and rudely slammed the door in Jerome's face. The young man sighed and sat down on the ground a few yards back from the door. He took the makeshift pack from his back and spread out his few belongings. From some stale Ken-cow cheese he had found at the ruined farmstead and some dried Ko-pods, he made his meal. As the sounds of night grew, so did Jerome's weariness. It had been an exhausting day. His eyes heavy, he lay down on his spare robe and soon was fast asleep.

He awoke to the sound of the Master clattering about in the hut. The sun was not yet up, but the largest of Kensho's moons flooded the woodscape with its blue light. Jerome broke fast with the last of his cheese and Ko-pods and then went to the little stream that nearby trilled its way downhill. He splashed water over his face. The clear cold of it woke him thoroughly.

Now what to do? He decided it would be useless to approach the Master again, demanding to be allowed to study with him. He would simply have to play a waiting game, staying around, doing things, until the Master came to accept him by the mere fact of his presence. It would take time. But time was about the only asset Jerome had.

When the Master finally came from his hut, stretching and yawning, wearing the same home-spun robe as yesterday, he ignored the young man sitting patiently a few yards away. As the old man mumbled about the edge of the clearing, looking for small twigs to start a fire, Jerome let the Litany of Passivity wash through his mind, clearing and calming it, schooling him to patience, to acceptance.

After the Master re-entered his hut and shut the door with a bang, the young man rose and went into the woods. For a while all was silent in the little clearing, but for the buzzing of the Ko-bees and the occasional cry of a tree lizard. Eventually a huffing and crackling of something coming through the woods shattered the peace. The next instant, Jerome appeared, almost invisible beneath a pile of dry wood he had gathered. He staggered across the clearing to the hut and dumped the pile next to the door. Then he returned to his place and resumed his meditation.

The sun rose higher and spilled a sideways glance into the small clearing on the slope of the Mountain. The Master emerged from the hut once more and shuffled off across the open space and into the forest. Jerome rose and followed on soundless feet, more the Master's shadow than his companion. A short walk through the woods brought them to another clearing where the Master tended his garden. Silently, the two of them bent over the rows, weeding and tending the plants. The sun beat down equally on their heads, bringing sweat to both brows. Noon came and the old man left the clearing and the garden. He walked into the woods to where the stream wandered about. After drinking he gathered a few handfuls of berries and wild fruit pods, then squatted by the side of the stream, munching his frugal fare, watching the young man who copied his every move.

Finishing his meal, the Master rose and began stalking determinedly through the woods as though on his way to an important appointment. Behind him, Jerome scurried to keep up. Eventually the striding old man and the scurrying young one came to a place in the forest where nothing grew but a huge Ko tree. Jerome craned his neck and tilted back his head. The top of the tree was lost amid the confusion of its own branches. At its base, the trunk was easily forty feet around.

Close to the base, in the deep shade of the branches, the Master took his seat, facing outwards. He crossed his legs, adjusted his hands, regulated his breathing and went into the meditation state known as "not-here-not-there." Seating himself about two yards in front of the Master, facing inwards, Jerome adopted a similar posture and went into the meditation state known as "waiting-with-awareness."

For hours the two were still while the forest went about its life.

As the sun's rays reddened with the coming of evening, the old man arose silently from his position and walked back to the garden. Trailed by Jerome, he picked a few vegetables and returned to the hut. Again he slammed the door, denying the young man access. Jerome made a cold meal of the vegetables he had harvested, washed down with even colder water from the stream.

Eventually, since the Master did not venture forth again from the hut, Jerome lay down and went to sleep.

In this way many days passed softly, hardly leaving any trace behind them, so similar were they all.

Suddenly one morning everything changed forever.

Jerome awoke knowing that someone was standing over him. He opened his eyes the barest slit, keeping his body relaxed and ready. Feet. With ragged old sandals. Knotted, tough calves. The hemline of a homespun robe.

It was the Master. Jerome opened his eyes fully and sat up.

The Master squatted, peering into his eyes, his face only a few inches from Jerome's.

"Who are you?" Abrupt. Harsh.

"Jerome."

"What are you?"

"A Seeker."

"What do you seek?"

"The Way of the Sword."

"Why?"

The question reverberated through Jerome's entire being. Why, why, why, why, why, why . . . . . ? Because the Sword had shattered his life. Because the Sword had murdered his parents. Because the Sword had shaped his life in the Brotherhood. Because the Sword had led him up this Mountain to this very spot. Because the Sword might be the key to setting his race free from the Mushin. Because the Sword represented Death and Life and Despair and Hope. Because the Sword . . . . why, why, why, why, why. . . . . ? Why? A million "Becauses."

And yet, and yet . . . Why? Was there any answer to that question? Were "becauses" answers? Why? Was he here to save his race? Who or what had appointed him Savior? Was he here to avenge his parents? Was there any way to achieve that revenge?

Why?

The Master stared hard at the lad, his eyes burning deep, deep into the mists of confusion so thinly disguised in Jerome's own eyes. Why? The Master waited. Jerome must answer, something, anything.

And Jerome knew the answer was crucial. He knew his whole future hung on it. He knew the

Master would accept or reject him on the basis of it.

He had no answer.

"I don't know."

With a grunt, the Master rose and stood looking down at him. "Well, at least you're honest. You don't know the reason why you want to study the Way. Or rather, you know too many reasons. Your mind is like a flock of birds, each bird a reason, each seeking to roost on a single limb. As soon as one settles, another lands and jostles the first off the limb."

Confused, Jerome blurted, "What must I do? Must I allow only one bird to land? Must I get rid of the others?"

"Rid yourself of all the birds. And the limb."

The young man stared blankly at the old one. Finally the Master sighed, "Enough of birds. There are no birds.

"So. The long and short of it is you wish to study the Way of the Sword. For whatever reasons.

"There is danger here. Many are the paths one may follow on the Way. Some are broad and gentle. Others follow the high, rocky places. Great chasms yawn on all sides. And one slip plummets the seeker into the depths of the Madness.

"For on all paths, on the Way, the Mushin lurk. They are always ready to seize on any emotion not hidden, to reinforce it, to feed it back into the mind, thus starting a spiralling growth that drives the mind to raving Madness. Then as the mind dies, they feast.

"This," the old man continued, as if reciting a

litany, "is what they did to us when first we arrived here on Kensho. We were unprepared for them. Our surveys of the planet showed no evidence of their existence, no sign of higher life, no mark of civilization, nothing but primeval wilderness. So satisfying was the very vision of it hanging there in space, that Admiral Nakamura named it "Kensho" after one of the stages of Enlightenment.

"Then the Pilgrims landed at First Touch, far off down the Mountain, down the Valley, across the Plain, by the Sea, and everyone went mad, tearing at each other, murdering, maiming. Like vicious, wild animals. It was the Madness. It blew the Colony apart and scattered the raving, killing, human debris across the landscape."

The Master looked down at the young man. "I know you've heard all this. But you must hear it again. You must know what you risk. For you risk what they risked. The Madness. True, you have defenses they did not. You have the Passivity, the disciplines and exercises the Grandfathers taught our race. And by now, you may even have some sort of natural defenses, developed by the force of natural selection and the terrific pressures of the last seven generations. But still, the risk is real."

Jerome swallowed hard. "I know this. Still I would be a Seeker of the Way even if the Madness were inevitable. I can do no else."

For a moment the old man stood there gazing down at the young one, sadness filling every wrinkle on his weatherbeaten face. Then the sadness melted and sternness replaced it. "Very well," he said brusquely, "Come with me." He turned on his heel and stalked to the hut.

The young man followed. The hut consisted of three small rooms. One, barely more than a large closet, was without a door. It held at least a hundred sheathed swords, scattered and piled about in no apparent order. On top of the pile, Jerome noticed the six swords the Master had collected from the Ronin slain down the valley. The second room, likewise doorless, contained a rough pallet and a grimy blanket. The final room, larger than the other two, held a crude fireplace hung with cooking utensils, several bins for storing vegetables, assorted cushions, and the Master's sword, hanging on the wall opposite the hearth.

From a corner, the Master took a handmade broom and held it out to Jerome. "Sweep the hut. Then prepare us breakfast."

Chapter VII

ONCE AGAIN THE days followed the sun over the horizon like identical beads on a string. There was no sense in counting them, no logic to keeping track. To number each would have been to differentiate it from all others, to name this the Day the Tree Lizards Sang, and that the Day They Didn't, one the Day that Brought Rain, another the Day the Sun Shone. But it was useless, for even the differences repeated themselves, and even the similarities changed. It was a rhythm that needed nothing to complete or complement it.

Jerome's life was the same. He swept the hut, gathered firewood, carried water, tended the garden, cooked the meals, meditated, and then began the round again. Soon it became impossible, or at least unnecessary, to determine which was the first act and which the last. As long as one followed the other, order was preserved.

At first, Jerome was perfectly happy. To be in the Master's presence was enough. But as the days passed through weeks and into months, he became fretful. When was the Master going to teach him the Way of the Sword? Never once did the old man so much as touch the sword that hung on the hut's wall. Never did he even look in the smaller room filled with conquered swords. And his conversation was solely on matters domestic or personal.

Jerome's unease grew into dissatisfaction. He began to drop hints. He took some of the swords out of the small room and cleaned them until their blades shone. He made a wooden bokken and went through the motions of the practice forms, the katas, he had studied with Father Ribaud at the Brotherhood.

The Master ignored him.

Jerome's dissatisfaction grew into anger. He commandeered a real sword from the storeroom and practiced his cuts on the air. He drilled his draws and repeated his katas with the naked blade.

The Master merely complained that the garden was not adequately weeded.

Anger fed on itself and became a barely concealed rage. The young man took to walking through the woods with his sword, slashing at small saplings and branches to test the trueness of his cut: it was ragged; his blade waffled, and the edges were not clean.

The Master could not help but notice such wanton destructiveness. Yet his only comment was to remark that if Jerome wished to cut green wood to smoke meat, an axe would be more appropriate.

The day came when Jerome could contain himself no longer. He fought for control all morning, all through the weeding, all through meditation. When evening finally came he was beside himself. He decided to confront the Master.

By the time they had finished dinner, Jerome had inflamed his courage by stoking it with his anger. Abruptly, with no preamble (other than weeks of nervous fidgeting) he launched into his complaint. "Master. Why have you not taught me the Way?"

The Master looked up, mock surprise written across his face. "Not taught you? I? How is that so? Have I not let you sweep the hut, fix the meals? Have you not weeded the garden, carried water, collected firewood?"

"But . . . but . . . You never show me any techniques, never drill me in my kata. You never teach me any advanced techniques or new kata. You never even speak of the Sword and the Way!"

"Techniques? Katas? Words? What have such things to do with the Way? The sword is not the Way. It is but a way to the Way."

"Why do you seek so far off for the Way? Do you think to find it like some rare mountain flower, hidden in a cleft in some isolated crag? The Way is here. It is in the broom, the firewood, the vegetables. It is in eating when you are hungry, sleeping when you are tired."

"But the Sword! I am not learning the Sword!

How can there be a Way of the Sword without the Sword?"

"The Sword is the least important part of the Way of the Sword. He who has truly learned the Way of the Sword does not even carry a Sword. But I see what the problem is. You wish to become a Swordsman, and you confuse this with the Way of the Sword."

"How can they be different?"

"When the sun shines in the sky, you cannot grasp it. When the moon reflects in a pool, you cannot grasp it. Are they both then the same?"

The young man looked puzzled. "I don't understand."

The Master chuckled. "That I am aware of, Seeker. You do not understand.

"Very well, then, Seeker. You wish to be trained as a Swordsman. It is not the Way. But all in all, it is as much a way to the Way as sweeping the hut. It is a harder way, with much greater danger. It is a longer way, too. But, very well, if that is your wish, so be it. I will begin training you as a Swordsman tomorrow. You will have all you wish, training, exercises, words. May you live through it." The old man yawned, stretched, and then ambled off to his room. In a moment, he was blissfully sleeping.

Hours later, the excited Seeker finally managed to follow his example.

The next morning, Jerome fixed breakfast as usual and then went out into the dew-wet woods to gather firewood and pick a few berries and Ko-pods. As he wandered about, his excitement began to grow. The Master had promised! He had promised to train him! He wondered what new forms he would learn, what wondrous techniques he would master. Perhaps someday the Master would even teach him the techniques he had used against the six Ronin! How hard he would study! He would spend hour after hour perfecting every cut and stroke! The Master would be proud of him, just as Father Ribaud had been proud.

Without warning he felt a tremendous blow, a shattering pain, between his shoulder blades. He was thrown to the ground by its force, the wood and berries flying in all directions. Even though surprised, he remembered to roll as he hit, ready to spring to his feet and confront his attacker. Before he could even complete his roll another blow caught him on the side of the head. Dizzy, he tried to rise, holding his hands above his head to protect himself. A stunning slam doubled him over. With hands raised, his stomach had been wide open.

The blows rained down. Jerome rolled and scrabbled this way and that, trying to avoid them. His head spinning, his eyes filled with tears of pain, he tried to rise and face his tormenter. But there was never a moment's let up, never a chance to even call out to the Master for help, much less time to stand and run or fight.

All his training was of no avail. He tried to block the blows, but wherever he moved his hands, the attacker struck the place they had just left. With a terrible surge of effort, he managed to come to his knees, then staggered to his feet. Turning toward the blows, he faced his attacker. Ignoring the battering his ribs took, he raised his hands to shield his head, to wipe one eye clear, to see.

The Master struck him on the shoulder so strongly that he collapsed back to his knees. Then the Master lashed out again at his head and flattened him.

The Master!

The shock of that made the battering his body was taking seem mild by comparison. It was a shock to the seemingly invulnerable controls he had built over a lifetime. He felt the walls that kept his emotions in and the Mushin out weakening, crumbling. Fear, stark terror, battered at them from inside as strongly as the Master smashed from outside. The Master!

It was beyond logic, beyond understanding. The Master had promised to train him. And now the Master was beating him to death. Why? Why?

Exhausted, sobbing with pain, humiliation, grief, anger, horror, he felt the ultimate terror. He felt the tingling presence of Mushin rushing to investigate this source of emotions, this feast of fear. And he knew he was defenseless. Defenseless against the Mushin! Defenseless against the Madness! With a thin whimper of futility, he tried to hold in his emotions. But it was no good, it wouldn't work, his control was gone, smashed by the Master's club. As his anguish swept up in a cresting wave, the Mushin and the Master's club swept downward.

He didn't know which arrived first. For there

was a roaring flash and total blackness.

To his utter surprise, Jerome awoke. For a few moments, he lay there, wondering at it, gently testing his mind to search for signs of the Mushin. Nothing.

He tried to move. Pain smashed into him from every direction. There wasn't anything that didn't hurt. He sat up and the world began to flow in different directions at the same time. He waited, and eventually the whirling and swooping stopped and the world settled into its accustomed orbit. Holding his throbbing head, he peered about. The Master was gone. There was calm in the woods.

He checked his body. Nothing seemed to be broken, though a rib or two might be cracked and he was a mass of bruises. He stood. While he waited for the world to stabilize again, he once more searched for Mushin.

He checked his mind. The walls of control were still there. They hadn't been destroyed any more than his body had been. But they ached, too.

Gods! What a beating! Worse than any he had ever suffered at the hands of the older Sons in his early years at the Brotherhood. He felt a mixture of anger and humiliation rising, bitter at the back of his throat. The Master had done this. Why? Did the old man hate him so? What had he done to deserve such treatment? He had gathered firewood, cooked the old man's vegetables, weeded the garden, hauled water, swept, done everything. Why had the Master treated him this way?

The old man must hate him. That could be the only reason. The Master had never had any intention of teaching Jerome the Way of the Sword. He had only wanted a servant. Jerome's insistence that he be trained had undoubtedly angered the old man. Now he was trying to drive Jerome away.

Calmer now, the young man thought it through. The Master hated him, hated him badly enough to beat him senseless and nearly kill him, opening him up to the Mushin. He wanted Jerome to run, to leave in fear, to escape from the beatings so he would not have to teach him the Way.

But Jerome thought, I can hate, too. Ever since the night he had watched helplessly as his family had been massacred, he had known what hatred really was. He had taken hatred into the very depths of his being, and it had become the major fuel for his existence. It had stoked the fires of his determination in the practice yards of the Brotherhood. It had strengthened his decision to follow the Way of the Sword, to challenge even the Brotherhood and the Grandfather, if necessary, to achieve his goal.

The Master cannot drive me away, the young man thought, with a hatred so old, a rage so ancient, it went back to the very dawning of human consciousness. I will stay. I will learn. I will triumph.

Slowly, like an ancient, he picked up his scattered firewood, giving the berries up as lost, and staggered through the woods to the hut and the clearing.

The Master was sitting in the sun next to the hut,

waiting. He smiled secretly and sadly as the young man unloaded the wood and threw a defiant glance his way.

The beatings became more and more frequent as the days went by. Jerome lived in constant fear of the whistling club which struck him down any time, any place. He was in even greater dread of the Mushin which lurked around constantly now, drawn by the fear he leaked, waiting for him to lose control so they could feast on his shattered mind. The Madness loomed larger than it ever had in his life. Larger even than the club-wielding Master.

Jerome never knew when or from where the next blow would come. The anticipation was almost as agonizing as the actual beatings. He was at a fever pitch of expectancy every moment of the day. It could happen while he was cooking. Or when he was bending down weeding. Or in the woods. Or even during meditation. One night he awoke in agony to find the Master standing over him in the dark, swinging and connecting by sheer chance.

His nerves frayed, then tattered. His hands began to shake. He was constantly nauseous, unable to keep his food down. Fear was his companion, his shadow, always at his side. The sound of its jabbering kept him from sleep at night, woke him if he snatched at rest during the day. Closer and closer he came to exhaustion, to defeat, to the Mushin, to death by the Madness. Yet always at the last moment he rallied, drawing energy from some source deep within, from his hatred, from the dark place at his center.

Slowly, ever so slowly, Jerome began to find little clues to the Master's lurking presence. A whisper of wind where nothing should be stirring, a shadow out of place, a sudden silence among the tree lizards. His senses extended themselves, not consciously, not purposely, but naturally. It was never anything he could command. If he held a clue up for examination by his mind, it melted and disappeared. He simply had to accept them, experience them, without thinking, without judging.

One morning, coming back from gathering wood, he approached the hut with extra caution. There had been no sign of the Master in the woods. As he came to the door, he hesitated. Something tasted, felt, seemed wrong. Uneasiness spread about him like ripples from a stone thrown in a calm pond.

Shaking his head, he tried to bring himself under control. He looked around carefully, noting each thing in the clearing, studying the hut, cataloging, comparing, calculating. There was nothing, his rational mind said. Something, came a dim echo from the dark at the center of his being.

Nothing, he repeated more firmly, asserting control. Nothing. I'm just nervous, tense. He shook himself again to loosen his stiff muscles and entered the hut.

A tremendous blow across the shoulders sent him sprawling to the floor. He twisted as he fell to see the Master leaping at him. "Fool!" the old man shrieked. "Fool of a fool! You sensed something wrong and yet you entered!" The club rose fell in time with the words. Jerome writhed about, trying to escape the blows. "You knew, and yet you let your knowledge be denied! Fool! Fool!"

Time passed. The beatings continued. Jerome kept no track of the days, for no one wishes to remember pain and humiliation. His hatred burned like a fierce flame deep inside his mind, shielded from the hovering Mushin by his iron control, providing him the energy he needed to keep going. He ate like a wild animal, gulping his food in quick snatches, ever on the alert. He slept and worked and walked and even meditated in the same way.

Then one day all the little clues connected and just before the club struck, Jerome knew it was coming. Desperately, he twisted to avoid it. And succeeded! The Master smiled to himself as he walked away.

Jerome extended his consciousness fully. He continuously sampled the environment with his awareness, on watch, ever testing the wind, listening for the false note, the jarring accent, the unnatural motion. He sank his being fully into the world around him, letting it wash over his consciousness, becoming one with it, extending himself out and out and out to become the very atoms of the air. If they vibrated with the passage of a body, he vibrated. He grew into an awareness that transcended mere observation, mere discrimination, mere reflex. It came from the center of his being, from someplace beyond the self, and flowed outward to encompass and blend with the All until there was no longer any outside or inside.

More and more often, as time passed, the Master's blows landed on thin air.

Chapter VIII

WHY? WHY DOES he do this? thought Jerome. He readjusted his aching body to better fit the bumps and hollows of the forest floor. He pressed against the coolness, sucking up what refreshment it offered. Why? he thought again, realizing his mind was still too muddled, too recently returned to consciousness to yield a coherent answer.

Clarity returned quickly. But it came alone, without an answer to his confusion. It just didn't make sense. Most of the time the Master was quite normal, at times positively jolly.

But then suddenly he would attack, trying to beat the young man senseless. At first, it had appeared to Jerome as if the old man hated him and was trying to scare him off, to drive him away so he wouldn't have to teach him the Way of the Sword as he had promised. That must be wrong. Months had passed. It was obvious to anyone by now that Jerome could not be driven off in that manner. If the Master hated him, Jerome knew how to respond with a hate of his own. He could hold his ground with no trouble. His hate gave him the strength.

Yet the Master, aside from the continued beatings, did not seem to hate Jerome at all. It did not show in any of his other actions. Indeed, if anything showed it was a stern affection.

Confused, Jerome reviewed it all again. If he hates me, I can hate back and it's a draw. If he doesn't hate me, how can I hate him? But if he doesn't hate me, why does he beat me so brutally? And if I don't hate him where will I get the strength to live through the beatings? Around and around it went.

He thought back to the beating he had just received. For many weeks he had suffered very little because he had become so adept at dodging the Master's blows. Now and then, however, a solid smash had landed. Jerome had reasoned that if he had a stick or a club of his own, he would be able to block the Master's club rather than just dodging it. It seemed to follow that in such fashion he might avoid being struck altogether and force the old man to recognize the situation as a standoff.

So he had scoured the woods for a likely club of his own. One morning while gathering wood, he found it. Holding it, checking its merit, he swung it a few times, then, satisfied, he had stuck it in his belt and headed back to the hut.

He never got there. Suddenly the Master had leaped from behind a tree.

Jerome dodged the first blow, then fumbled briefly and pulled his weapon out. The Master grinned wolfishly when he saw what the youth was attempting. "Fool!" he chortled with undisguised glee. "Fool! You'd fight back? Does the treelizard stand and fight the Ken-wolf?" With a quick feint, he forced Jerome to open himself up. Then with contemptuous nonchalance, he knocked the club from the young man's hand. Astounded, the Seeker made just the slightest move to retrieve it. Seeing what he waited for, the Master struck, knocking him to the forest floor, leaping instantly to follow up with a murderous pounding attack.

"Fool," the Master preached as he struck, his monologue punctuated with the grunts of his victim's agony, the twack of his weapon, and his own snorts of effort. "You pull back. You snuff out your awareness with your ego. You let go of the world and hold a broken branch. You bring your mind to a halt with a piece of wood, even following it as it sails away. Your mind abides in the branch, it moves away from you, leaving you defenseless. The branch cannot save you unless you hold it as before you held the world. You must let go of the branch before you can hold it. Flow. Be immovable. Or die." Finishing the sermon and the beating, the Master had strode off into the forest, laughing mightily.

Jerome's body ached anew at the memory. Trembling, he raised himself to his knees. His hand came in contact with the club. He pulled back in instant revulsion. What a beating!

His hand crept forward again, like a bruised, lost spider. Fingers curled around the wood. Hold the club as I hold the world, he thought. Let go of the branch so I can hold it. What did the Master mean? How did he "hold" the world?

He didn't hold the world. He simply let his mind flow into the world and let the world flow through his mind. It was easy. The world lived and moved. Things changed, the wind blew. He could float along with the current. When things were right, his mind was right. When anything was wrong, he knew it without checking. And reacted.

But a piece of wood? How could he let his mind flow through a piece of wood? How could a branch flow through his mind?

I don't understand, he puzzled. I don't understand anything.

More days, more weeks, more beatings taught him the secret. He didn't think of it anymore. Pay no attention to the club and it becomes part of you. Focus on it and you lose it.

Soon he was blocking the Master's blows as often as he was receiving them. A great pride filled him. Soon I can hold my own with the Master! One day he came back alone from weeding the garden, his club in his hand, stalking warily through the woods. As he reached the hut and was about to enter the door, he paused. There was something wrong. He recognized the feeling. He had felt it before. And received a terrible beating for ignoring it. This time he was ready, alert for any trickery. His club poised for an instant counter, he stepped through the door.

But the blow didn't come from above. It came from below. The Master had been lying next to the door, waiting. As Jerome stepped through, anticipating a blow from behind, the Master struck up, hitting the young man in the groin. With a groan, Jerome crashed to the floor, unconscious. The Master beat him anyway, bellowing the while, "Triple damned fool! You knew something was wrong! You knew it! Yet you trusted your skill to save you! Triple fool! Though you are unconscious, you hear me! Remember!"

There came a morning when the Master was unable to land a single blow. Jerome twisted and blocked every effort the old man made. Finally realizing it was a draw, the old man stopped and Jerome stood looking anxiously across the gulf that yawned between them.

"Hmmmm," began the Master. "Not bad. And you've had the good sense not to try to go on the offensive. It would have been disaster, just as when you first tried active defense. Know that to attack you must encompass the enemy just as you encompass the world and your own weapon. You must make yourself one with him, one with his sword. You do not fight against him. You fight with him, letting him make a mistake. There is no thought. He makes a mistake, breaks the rhythm you have established between you, and is defeated by himself."

Jerome nodded. "I am not ready for that yet."

"No. Not yet. But you would do for most fights, with most Ronin bands. And I wager there are few Fathers you could not master."

Keeping his eyes on the Master, Jerome bowed in mock gratitude. "Thank you."

"You are most welcome." And the old man spun about and walked off.

A rainstorm was coming. Jerome stood once again outside the hut, feeling the wrongness all about him. He looked in the door, moving around to get the best possible view. Nothing to be seen. Yet it felt hostile, incorrect, incomplete. He pondered. Doubtless it was a trap. He could trust to his skill and hope to come off well. After all there were only so many angles the Master could strike from. This time he would consider them all. He started to enter, then hesitated. Still, though, the Master was tricky. He might have a new trap.

A light rain began to fall. I'd best go in—but as cautiously as possible—he thought. Then he stopped himself. No. It was a trap. He would be beaten. Better to be wet than beaten. With a great show of indifference, he sat down on the sodden ground and composed himself, folding his dripping robe carefully about his feet so he could rise quickly if necessary.

He waited. After a time the Master came to the door and motioned him in. "Come. You're wet enough." With dignity Jerome rose and walked slowly and calmly to the door. He stopped. Everything felt all right. With a nod he entered. A silent smile played over the Master's face.

That night, and for every night following, the Master cooked his own meals. He no longer ordered Jerome about. The old man even went into the forest to help gather firewood. All attacks ceased.

But Jerome was still seething with bitterness. So many beatings, so many humiliations, and never an opportunity to strike back. Not even once. How sweet revenge, even one little blow, would be!

A plan began to form in the young man's mind. The Master had always managed to catch Jerome unaware, and, at the beginning, unarmed. If he managed to catch the Master the same way, he could achieve his revenge.

Patience had to be his guide. And careful observation. He watched the Master closely to see what would be the best moment. Catching the old man asleep would be too cowardly. Outside it would be hard to sneak up, for the old man's senses were as sharp, or even sharper, than Jerome's. The hut, then, inside the hut. There was no way he could lay a trap as the Master had done since the Master always entered first. Some other time, then.

Jerome kept his club close and waited. One night, on the spur of the moment, he realized his chance had come. The Master was at the fireplace, cooking his vegetables for dinner. He had taken the pot off the grate, lifted the lid, and was tasting the contents to see if it was ready. His eyes were closed, savoring the flavor, judging, concentrating in the sheer pleasure of taste.

Stealthily, Jerome crept up behind the unsuspecting cook. With utter calm, utter silence, he lifted his club and struck downward at the bent back.

Revenge!

Jerome was never really too sure exactly what happened next. He saw the Master turn as the club fell. There was no look of surprise or fear in his eyes. If anything, there was the slight quirk of a smile on his lips.

Everything seemed to move in slow motion. As if he had all the time in the world, the old man lifted the pot lid he held in his hand and interposed it between his head and the club. With a ringing crash, the club shattered, leaving Jerome's hands numb with the shock of impact. The lid did not stop. It kept moving up toward the young man towering over the bent old one. Up it rose, up toward his face. It was the last thing he saw for some time.

When he came to, Jerome instantly knew his nose was broken and his jaw was probably cracked. Several teeth felt loose. He spat blood and looked around. It was a mistake. His head refused to move, so great was the pain the attempt aroused.

Finally his eyes stopped watering and the agony subsided. Quietly, he thanked whatever Gods inhabited the slopes of the Mountain that he was still alive, and prayed that he had suffered no serious concussion.

"Ah," commented a sardonic voice, "the Young Avenger awakes." A cold splash of water hit him. "Ah. Even more awake now. Perhaps even rational, at last."

Jerome looked up and saw the Master looking down. "How does your head feel, Seeker? Still there?"

Confusion for a moment. "How . . .? what . . .?"

The old man chuckled. "Oh, come now. I didn't hit you that hard! Surely you remember what a fool you were!"

It all came back in a flood of shame. Revenge. He had tried to strike the Master in revenge! He sat up. "I . . . I . . ."

Looking solemn, the Master knelt next to him. "Is there no room in you for anything but revenge, lad? Revenge against the Ronin for killing your parents, revenge against the Mushin for the Madness, revenge against me for teaching you what you wanted to learn in a manner you didn't like? Is that all there is at your core? Revenge?"

Tears came to Jerome's eyes. "I don't know. I don't know."

The old man sighed. "Better you had stuck with the broom, Seeker. Eventually you would have come to the same place, anyway. It would have been better.

"In a way, I have failed. I should have refused to let you go beyond the broom. It was so obvious you didn't understand. You came here seeking a weapon to fight the Mushin. You thought the Way of the Sword would provide it.

"Listen, Seeker, listen. You see the Mushin as

your enemy. You see them as external to yourself and your race. So you look for some way to destroy them to free your race.

"Know, Seeker, know. The enemy is not without, but within. The Mushin but take what is there and amplify it. They create nothing. Anything they make a man into he already is. They make us what we are, Seeker. They are a magnifying mirror held up to us.

"Understand, Seeker, understand. You are the enemy. Everything you do reflects your true nature, your real self. You have not studied the Way of the Sword. You have sought a weapon. You have sought to turn the Way to your ends, to make the Path follow your path. You must give up your path if you are to walk the Way.

"Hear me, Seeker. I give you a new Litany to replace that of Calmness. I give you the Litany of the Way.

> The Sword is the Mind.
> When the Mind is right,
>   the Sword is right.
> When the Mind is not
>   right, the Sword
>   is not right.
> He who would study
>   the Way of the Sword
>   must first study
>   the Way of his Mind."

Dazed by shock after shock, by word after searing word, Jerome recognized the Litany. It was the chant the Grandfather had used in an attempt to take over his mind so long ago! It was the same chant that had forced him to fight for his existence, that had caused the explosion of emotion, that had led him to strike and kill the alien ruler of the Brotherhood!

But this time it drove him inward, behind his walls of defense not to fight, but to flee ever downward into the center of his being. The question the Master had asked him that day— "Why?"—accompanied him on his journey through his own soul.

This was not the voyage he had made before. He did not pass the boundaries of Self. He did not see himself as a pathetic creature in a dark cell holding the crumpled head of a Grandfather in his hand. He did not float over the agony, the blackness, the void that was his Center. This time he plunged right in.

What the Master had said was true. He did live for revenge. He found himself once more sitting over his mother's body, muttering as he straightened her ravaged clothes, "I'll get you. I'll do it. I'll get you," over and over and over, making it a part of his being. When the older boys at the Brotherhood had beaten him behind the Refractory, he had done the same thing. And then carried out ingenious revenges. The day he had understood the plight of his race on Kensho, he had pledged revenge against the Mushin. Since then his entire life had been dedicated to achieving it.

It was true. Revenge did fill his inner core, his True Self.

No. Wait. There was more. There were the emotions that motivated the revenge. There was the love for his parents. There was the friendship, the sense of belonging he had felt even when being beaten by the older Sons. There was the hope that someday his race would be free once more.

Other things, too. The sheer joy of moving with the sword, his muscles singing, his breath ringing. The peace that sitting beneath the Ko tree brought. The warmth a smile from the Master kindled. And so much more.

It was all there. Only it had all been swept into the corners to make more room for the revenge. Or twisted and bent to make it fit the form of his revenge. He saw it all.

And suddenly he saw something else, too. It unfolded before him in all its simplicity, every look, every incident, every word. The Master's love.

Weeping, Jerome looked outward, through his eyes. The old man still knelt before him. "I . . . I understand. I struck at the Grandfather, unknowing, I struck at you, unknowing. Now I know.

"I know the dark chaos at my own Center. And I know the Light. The darkness must yield to the Light, and calmness must replace the chaos. When my Center is calm it will reflect the Light like still waters reflect the moons. And it will light the Way."

Slowly Jerome rose and stood tall. The Master rose with him. For a moment, the two men simply looked at each other. Then, calmly and gently, the Master spoke. "The time has come for you to go, Seeker. I have done all I can for you. No man can walk the Way for another. Each must find it for himself." The Master paused, his head cocked to one side, his eyes turned inward to search his own Center for something to say, something that would give Jerome guidance as he searched.

"You have walked the Way of the Sword, Jerome. But although you have learned to hold a sword, your journey is not yet over. Now you must learn to hold The Sword.

"For the Sword has many forms. One you know well. It is the Sword of Death."

Jerome nodded gravely. Yes, he knew the Sword of Death, the Sword carried by the Ronin, the Sword that killed, that took life and gave nothing in return.

The Master continued. "The Sword of Death is the sword used for fulfillment of ego desires. It consists of mere technique practiced for gain and satisfaction of the baser goals of human existence. It serves passion, greed, hate, evil.

"Opposite the Sword of Death is the Sword of Life. This sword may also bring death. But in doing so, it gives life. It serves the cause of Humanity, justice, love, goodness. The individual using it gains nothing for himself. The gain is always for others.

"But the Sword of Life cuts two ways. For when it is used correctly, it not only works outwardly, slaying its victim, but it works inwardly as well, transforming the swordsman himself, killing his ego, destroying his Desire. You have begun this transformation. You must follow it to its end.

"Beyond all this, there is a third Sword. But we

cannot talk of it. It transcends and creates the other two, yet it is everywhere congruent and coexistent with them. It contains both Good and Evil yet it is neither the one nor the other nor their sum. It simply Is. We call it the Sword of No Sword.

"Once you hold this Sword, you hold the answer to Nakamura's Koan, the Way that will free all men on Kensho from the Mushin and the Madness. By walking the Way of the Sword, you will eventually find this other Way, the Way of Kensho.

"This is your journey, Seeker, and it is a natural one, for you or for any man. For a man defends himself and his own as naturally as a stream seeks to join the Sea. But learn from the stream. It knows no Desire. Yet it cuts deep chasms and great valleys in its journey.

"Of course a man is not a stream. All men have Desire. But you can become like the stream if you hold your Desire as I have taught you to hold the sword. Then you will grasp the Sword of No Sword, the only weapon sharp enough to cut Nothing."

Jerome smiled and nodded. Three times he bowed his thanks, then turned and left without looking back.

As he walked across the clearing, through the Woods, down the Mountain, he thought of how his life seemed to be a series of departures. He had departed his mother's womb to enter the World. He had departed his home when the Ronin had destroyed it about him. He had departed the Brotherhood, fleeing in the night, when he had killed the Grandfather. And now he departed again. But this time he went willingly, on his own. And he knew that before him lay the Way and the future of his race.

Chapter IX

JEROME WANDERED.

He journeyed slowly northward through the mountains. Within a few days, he reached a wide, forested valley that extended from the southwest to the northeast. From its position and size, he estimated it began somewhere amid the mountains to the south and ended by joining the vast valley of the Big Water which lay to the north. It was watered by a small river that wound around its floor, creating rich, open meadows on its way to the Big Water. If the river or the valley had a name, Jerome didn't know them. His education in the Brotherhood had not stressed geography, so this area was virgin territory to him.

From the mountain-edged rim of the valley he

had a magnificent view. Here and there, he noticed signs of human habitation. 'Steaders had built their homes in the meadows and clearings, but they were thinly spread. Much of the land was still quite wild.

The longer he looked at the green valley splashed amid the grey mountains, with the liquid ribbon that twisted down its length and the brown dots of 'steads scattered about, the surer he felt that it was an ideal location for his present task. He was on his own now, seeking the Way, trying to discover the answer to Nakamura's Koan. He believed the search would be inward, requiring long periods of solitary contemplation. That meant he needed to be alone as often as possible. Detachment from the flow of everyday life was necessary. Common existence must be held at arm's length. The thinly-settled character of the valley would provide the solitude he needed.

At the same time that the valley provided for his spiritual wants it could satisfy his physical ones as well. For he realized his body would require food and clothing and even shelter when the weather turned very bad. As much as he desired to be alone, occasional but regular contact with the mundane world would be essential. The scattered farmsteads provided the perfect combination of a chance to exchange his labor for the things he needed and an opportunity to be isolated whenever he wished.

The area had another advantage, one he didn't consciously formulate, but which hung in the background of his thoughts nevertheless. It was a long way from the Brotherhood near Waters Meeting. He didn't know if anyone from the Brotherhood would still be hunting him, after all these years, for the murder of the Grandfather. But it seemed unlikely that the search, or even word of the deed, would have penetrated this far from its point of origin. He felt he would be safe here.

Pleased, he made camp for the night, eating some wild fruits and vegetables he had gathered during his journey. Then he curled up in a hollow formed by a tree and a rock face and slept soundly. As the morning sun rose, Jerome descended into the valley.

For several months, he wandered slowly northwards, following the valley from farmstead to farmstead. Generally, he would approach a 'steader's cabin early in the morning, standing clearly in view until they had decided he wasn't dangerous. Then he would exchange the standard greetings and ask if there was any work to be done in exchange for food or clothing or a place to spend the night. The rest of the day, perhaps two, would be spent working steadily, helping the family catch up on a workload that was always too great to finish. The next morning, supplied with enough food to last a few days, he would bid the family adieu and be on his way. The system worked well. The farmsteads provided for the needs of his body and the empty forest between met the demands of his spirit.

Wandering, working, and spending his spare moments searching within himself, Jerome soon became known to the 'steaders of the valley. His earnest, quiet, gentle manner won him respect and acceptance wherever he went. Within a year, every 'stead in the valley was open to him any time he chose to stop by. The 'steaders were satisfied with the arrangement, for the young man worked hard and required very little in return for his labors. No one really understood what he was doing, but they really didn't care since they benefited by it.

Then the band of Ronin came

Jerome finished filling in the grave. It was the third this month. In it, he had buried the remains of a man, his wife, and their baby daughter. He had liked the family a great deal, especially the man, who was not much older than Jerome himself. The wife had always given him more than he had earned by his work, and the very robe he now wore had been sewn by her hands.

Sticking his spade into the ground, he looked down at his own hands. They were calloused, empty, helpless. He gazed up at the clouds silently gliding by. They were uncaring. These deaths meant no more than the death of a tree lizard.

Balling both fists, he stared back at his hands again. When? he cried to himself. When? How much longer must I search for the Way to stop all this? How many more must die before I can halt the slaughter and set men free?

He felt a light touch at his sleeve and realized his eyes were closed. Turning his head slightly, he looked down into the boy's upturned face. The eyes were large and round, moist with unshed tears held barely in check. "Jerome," the child said in a tight, controlled voice, "let me say good-bye alone, okay? You go over there and don't peek for a couple of minutes." When the young man looked uncertain, the boy's voice took on a slightly desperate edge of pleading. "It's okay. I won't cry or anything to bring the Mushin. I promise."

Reluctantly, Jerome moved away as requested, respecting the child's wish to make whatever farewell he could with his dead parents. Breaking his promise for just a moment, he stole a quick glance at the small figure that stood alone at the edge of the grave.

His mind was filled anew with the wonder of it. The boy, Tommy, the son of the 'steader, had been sitting, waiting for Jerome when he had come this morning. His first words, as he had stumbled through the charred ruins toward the young wanderer had been, "I knew you'd come, Jerome. They're all gone. But I knew you'd come." Then Tommy had broken down, all the pent-up grief and fear and rage pouring out in a sudden surge of tears. Wary of lurking Mushin, Jerome had quickly quieted the boy.

Jerome shook his head. He had questioned the lad as gently as possible to discover how it had happened. Tommy's memory was fuzzy. He remembered the first, frenzied moments as the Ronin had begun to break into the cabin and his mother had shoved him beneath the bed. From then on, his memory was a blank until he had come to with the cabin just beginning to burn around him.

The obvious parallel between Tommy's experience and the tragic events of his own childhood made the whole event seem even more miraculous. The inexplicable had happened again. And if it had happened twice, it could happen more often. Precisely how common was it?

Not very, he estimated, or I would have heard about it at the Brotherhood. I was the only one there with such a history, and my time there covered a span of some fifteen years. But of course, there could have been others in other Brother or Sisterhoods.

Tommy's voice interrupted his thoughts. "I'm ready, now." Nodding, he took the child's hand in his own and began to walk across the fields away from the grave and the ruins. Not wishing to embarass the boy, he refrained from looking down, noticing from the corner of his eye the way Tommy wiped furtively at his eyes several times.

They entered the woods, Jerome in the lead, and continued that way for a while until Tommy called out, "Hey, slow down. You walk too fast." Smiling, Jerome turned and complied. The boy's dirt- and tear-streaked face was calm. "Where are we going?" he asked as he caught up. "We gonna kill Ronin?"

"No," Jerome answered. "No, we're going to try to avoid the Ronin. There are five of them and some of them have sharp swords, Tommy. We're heading for the Chien's 'stead. They'll take you in for now."

"I want to stay with you, Jerome. You're my friend. The wood sword you made me burned. Can you make me a new one?''

Jerome stopped and reached down. He picked the child up and held him for a moment. Gods, he thought, how do you explain things to a five-year-old? ''Uhhhh, Tommy, buddy,'' he began, ''uhhhhh, look, you can't stay with me. I've got no home, see? No place for you to stay. I, uh, can't feed you, because I don't have a 'stead. I just wander around working for people, like I worked for your Daddy and Mommy. So I can't take care of you.''

The boy looked solemnly at him. ''That's ok, Jerome. I like to wander, too. I'll go with you, huh?''

''No. It's too dangerous. And I have things to do. You'll . . . you'll be better off with the Chiens. They're nice people.'' He put the boy down and began to walk again. Tommy remained silent and kept pace.

It took about two hours to get to the Chiens' 'stead. They were an older couple whose son had already set up his own 'stead, and whose daughter had been Called into the Sisterhood. Jerome was sure they would accept Tommy with open arms.

As he neared the meadow where their cabin was located, Jerome felt a growing sense of uneasiness. Slowing his pace and changing direction slightly, he decided to approach the place through a small arm of the woods which jutted out across the meadow toward it. Halfway through the trees, he stopped, then slowly sank to the forest floor pulling Tommy down with him, silently gesturing to the boy to remain still.

In a few moments, the reason for his intuitive caution appeared at the edge of the meadow. Ronin. Three of them. Only one of the three had a sword, the other two being armed with crude wooden clubs. It was obvious from their gestures that an argument was going on between them over who should possess the sword.

Suddenly the two who were carrying the cudgels leaped on the one with the sword. The first within range of the blade died, the steel deep within his breast. He twisted as he fell, however, trapping the blade so that the swordsman couldn't withdraw it in time to counter the attack of the second assailant. The cudgel came down with a solid thunk! and the Ronin's head split like a rotten melon. The victor ripped the sword from his fallen companion's chest and, without so much as a backwards look, ran howling off into the forest.

Shaken as much by the suddenness and brutality of the attack as by the narrowness of his escape, Jerome was several moments in gathering his wits about him. When he had calmed his mind again, he looked down at the boy. Tommy was trembling slightly, but was under control. Surprised anew at the strength of the child, Jerome helped him to his feet.

Turning to enter the meadow, Jerome still felt uneasy. Something was not right, even now. He looked over at the two bodies. They were quiet, dead. What could it be? he wondered. Carefully, he scanned the perimeter of the meadow.

For several more moments, he stood there, uncertain, unable to pin his feeling down to anything visible. Everything was quiet.

That was it! Everything was too quiet! Someone should be stirring, either Rudy or his wife Maggie. But there was no one!

Identifying the source of his unease, he moved swiftly across the meadow to the cabin. Cautiously, he pushed the door open. Strange! If anyone was within, the door would have been barred, he realized. The cabin was empty!

In a series of ever-widening circles, he swept the meadow for signs of the old couple. There was nothing anywhere but the bodies of the two Ronin. No signs of struggle. Nothing. The two 'steaders had simply vanished!

Could they have fled to a neighbor's 'stead, perhaps their son's, in fear of the Ronin who had been ravaging the valley? He entered the cabin again and searched it thoroughly. Nothing was missing, not even the things they would have taken with them for such a journey.

Utterly confounded, Jerome came out of the cabin and sat on the doorstep, his arm around young Tommy, who had dutifully trotted by his side throughout the entire investigation. "Not here, huh?" the boy asked quietly. "They went away, Jerome?"

He nodded. "Yes. They went away. But how? And why?" Could they have been surprised in the woods by the Ronin? he pondered.

Tommy sighed hugely. "I won't stay here now, Jerome. I'm too little to be here alone. I'll come with you now."

Jerome looked down at the little figure, hunched

against him. My God, he thought, what a miserable day it's been for him! Was I this brave about the whole thing when Ribaud found me at Waters Meeting? His heart went out to the boy. I'll find you a good home, he promised silently. The best there is.

He was so intent on comforting the little figure by his side that he didn't notice the larger one moving swiftly and silently across the meadow in their direction.

The figure, covered by a robe similar to that which Jerome wore, but with the hood up, stopped about twenty feet away and quietly watched the two sitting in the doorway. A moment later, Jerome's senses told him he was being watched, and he looked up. In one swift motion, he was on his feet, Tommy thrust out of the way into the cabin. Automatically, his hand reached for the sword he didn't carry. Weaponless! the thought hit him. But at least there's only one, he reassured himself.

Now he looked more closely at the figure standing in the sunlight. The face was invisible in the shadow cast by the hood. But there was no sign of a sword or any other weapon in the hands. The robe disguised the shape of its wearer, but Jerome had the distinct impression that the figure was slender, almost feminine, beneath the shapeless cloth.

All this had passed through his mind in the merest flash of time. Then his entire thought process was stopped dead by a light laugh which filled the meadow. The hood was thrown back by a flip of the figure's head, and Jerome saw the smiling features of a young girl! The merriment that hung in the curve of her full lips was reflected in her bright blue eyes. The high cheekbones, aquiline nose and dusky color of her skin tended to give her face a serious look, so that the contrast was oddly startling and charming. She shook her long black hair free of the folds of the hood and laughed again.

"Bravely done," she chuckled. "Aside from the fact that you seem to suffer from blindness and deafness, your reaction time is excellent. I'll bet I could have walked up and tromped on your toes before you even noticed me. Whom do I have the pleasure of startling half out of his wits, and what are you doing at my parents' farmstead?"

Jerome was so utterly nonplussed, he couldn't even formulate an answer. Luckily, Tommy was quick to the rescue. Stepping out from behind the young man, he said, "Hi. I'm Tommy. He's my friend, Jerome. Mom and Dad and Sis are dead now, so Jerome is taking care of me. We're going to wander all over the place and kill Ronin."

The girl bowed to Tommy. With a smile, she said, "Thanks, Tommy. Is your friend dumb as well as blind and deaf? And how do you plan to kill Ronin without a sword? Or does Jerome hope they'll die of laughter?"

His face red, Jerome found his tongue. "All right. Enough. I was bringing Tommy here for the Chiens to take care of. Since his parents were killed last night by Ronin. That answer your question?"

Now it was the girl's turn to be embarrassed. Her gaze faltered and fell to the ground. "Gods," she muttered, "I'm sorry. I didn't realize . . . I mean . . ."

Jerome shrugged. "Forget it. Did you say this is your parents' 'stead? The Chiens are your parents?"

Approaching and taking Tommy by the hand, she replied, "Yeh, I'm their daughter, Chaka. I don't know you, but then I've been away for a while."

"Sisterhood?"

Her eyes narrowed and a certain wariness came into her face. "Uh-huh. Sisterhood."

"That's right. They told me you'd been Called. About three years ago?"

The wariness deepened. She nodded silently.

Jerome nodded in turn. The girl was obviously hiding something and the something was obvious. If she'd been Called three years ago, she should still be in the Sisterhood. Noviate lasted for at least two years, followed by First Frame, Second Frame, and Third Frame. Only then was a Brother or Sister allowed outside the gates. That meant at least five to six years before an individual returned to the outside world. The first few trips were always in the company of a senior Father or Mother. Not only was Chaka unaccompanied, but she was two years early.

Even more damning was the fact that the girl had returned to her home. No Brother or Sister was ever allowed to visit their previous home or parents. The strain was too much and interfered with the calmness mandated by the Way of Passivity. Filial affection gave rise to all kinds of emotions, especially Desire.

Quite simply, the girl must have run away. That would explain why she traveled with her hood up. But even as he entertained the thought, Jerome realized it was unheard of. Brothers and Sisters did not run away! The reason was simple. If their minds became so unstable as to reach the point where they decided to flee, the Mushin sensed their inner turmoil and attacked, destroying them before they traveled two feet beyond their cell door.

Yet I fled, he reminded himself. And after a murder at that. So it is possible. Obviously so, since two who had done so were standing before each other at that moment.

Chaka's gaze was cool and defiant, but her body was poised tensely, ready for instant flight if he said the wrong thing or made the wrong move. There was no fear in her eyes, just caution. The girl had seen him pause and think and undoubtedly realized what his conclusion had been. She had no reason to expect his reaction to her secret would be favorable and was taking no chances. Jerome approved of her preparedness.

"Obviously you've figured it out," she said quietly. He nodded. "So? What are you going to do about it?" she demanded.

He shrugged his indifference, hoping to disarm her suspicions. "What do I care if you ran away from the Sisterhood? I've no great love for the system. I ran away myself."

Chaka nodded wisely, her body relaxing. "That explains why a man your age is neither on a 'stead raising brats or in a 'hood keeping the Mushin fed. I wondered about that 'wandering' bit. Ok," she smiled, "I guess we're even. Now, where are my parents?"

Jerome shrugged his shoulders again. "Don't know. Tommy and I got here about an hour ago. We saw three Ronin fight it out over a sword. When we knocked at the door, the cabin was empty. We've searched everywhere, but there's no sign of either Rudy or Maggie, nor of any struggle."

The girl looked quietly off into the distance, her gaze abstract, eyes unfocused. Jerome didn't know how to classify her look. It wasn't sorrow or joy or any emotion he knew of. She seemed calm, but absent. Finally her eyes came back into focus and her face regained its normal animation. "So," she began softly, "it happened before I could get back."

"What happened?" Jerome asked.

"They went off to die," she gently replied.

"Die?" Astonishment showed in his voice.

"Yeh. Figure it out. What with the Ronin killing and burning all over the valley right now, the Mushin are here in force following them around. If there's any one thing the Mushin love, it's the emotions surrounding human death. I guess fear of death is the most basic emotion we have, one we share with even the lowest forms of life.

"Anyway, the Mushin have probably passed by here several times recently with their Ronin, so they knew my parents were old and not too far from death. No sense in having the Ronin kill them. They don't have much to live for and wouldn't give off enough emotions to make the effort worthwhile. Better prey in younger families.

"But they probably left a sentinel to watch my folks and alert the rest when things started happening. Then they could all come and enjoy a free lunch, even if it wasn't very lavish.

"Dad and Mom may be old, but they're not stupid. They knew what was going on and didn't want any part of it. When they figured they didn't have much time left, they shielded their minds and got out. Better to die out in the woods than to die where the Mushin expect you to die and can find you. Maybe you don't die in bed, but at least you go in dignity, free of the Mushin and the Madness."

Gesturing toward the surrounding forest, Jerome asked incredulously, "You mean that Rudy and Maggie are out there someplace, alone, dying?"

The girl nodded solemnly, then said, "Not alone. They have each other. And more important, they have the freedom to die in peace."

"But . . . but" he waved his arms helplessly, his face clearly showing his inner distress, "We've got to do something, got to go find them or something."

"Why? So we can lead the Mushin to them? Forget it, Jerome. They may be your friends, but they're my parents. I know them and love them—enough to respect their decision. They did what's right. Besides, now Rudy takes his secret with him to his grave."

"Rudy? Secret? What are you talking about?"

"Nothing. Forget it. It's done." She looked at Tommy. "We've got bigger problems. Living ones. What are you going to do with Tommy now?"

"Tommy," he replied, "Well, yes, Tommy. Uh . . . maybe I'll take him to your brother's 'stead."

She shook her head. "He's got three kids already. Doug is strong enough to handle the extra emotional load of another kid, but his wife isn't."

"Well, there are other 'steads. I'll find one that will take him in."

"Yeh. And you're just going to wander around with a little kid, through Ronin infested forests, until you do. Nice sword you've got. You'll need it," she replied sarcastically.

"Ummmmmm," mused Jerome.

"Hey, look, I'm going to stay here," Chaka announced. "I'd be happy to have Tommy around for company. He'd sort of balance out the family, so to speak."

Jerome just stared at the girl. He simply couldn't keep up with the way her mind flashed and darted from one surprise to the next. "You're going to stay here?" he parroted.

"Yeh. It's my 'stead by right of inheritance. I left the Sisterhood to come back, and now that I'm here, I'm going to stay."

"But a woman alone on a 'stead . . .?" Jerome didn't even know how to complete the thought it was so unusual.

Chaka snorted. "Pooh. I'm as strong as you. Well, maybe not quite. But I can take care of myself. I'm 'stead born and raised. I know as much about Ken-cows and crops as anybody. And Tommy will help me."

"Sure," piped up Tommy. "I'll help, Jerome. Chaka can be the Mommy and you can be the Daddy."

The girl laughed at Jerome's embarrassed expression. Completely at a loss for words, the young man just stared from one of them to the other. Finally he blurted out, "Uh, no, no, I can't be the Daddy. I've got things to do. I . . . I . . . can't be a 'steader.

"But, look, Chaka, just you and Tommy . . . What about Ronin? And the heavy work? And . . ."

"I know how to avoid the Mushin and the Ronin. So does Tommy, as he just proved. They won't find us, except by sheer chance. I'll take that risk. As for the heavy work, why you can stop by now and then in your wanderings and help us, just like you helped Mom and Dad. We'll be happy to save things up for you.

"And as for it being just Tommy and me," she continued with a triumphant look at Jerome, "that just shows how observant you are, Wanderer." She put her hand to her mouth, turned, and blew two quick, shrill whistles toward the trees on the other side of the meadow. Immediately, two small figures appeared and ran toward them. Jerome stared in astonishment as a boy and girl, about nine years old and obviously brother and sister, came to a breathless halt next to Chaka.

"This is Misako," she indicated the girl who bowed her greeting, "and this is Obie," with a gesture toward the boy.

"That's short for Obadiah," the boy said with a curt bow.

"They're survivors, like Tommy. I found them way north of here and they came with me. Right through all the Ronin. They'll do just fine here."

Looking from one shining and determined face to the other, Jerome recognized defeat when he saw it. He shrugged his shoulders, "Who am I to say you can't stay here? If you're all crazy enough to try, that's your business. I'll drop by from time to time to check on you and help with the work. Like I did for Maggie and Rudy. Like I do for everyone." With that, he turned on his heel and began walking toward the trees.

"Sure you don't want some breakfast?" Chaka's voice followed him. He could hear the laughter in the words and it irritated him. But it also made him feel warm.

Chapter X

THE RONIN DISAPPEARED from the valley as suddenly as they had appeared. Relative peace, if not security, settled over the area.

Jerome continued his wandering, but found that he unconsciously tended to center his movements around the 'stead where Chaka and the children lived.

The unorthodox household thrived. Little Tommy turned out to be a herdsman par excellance. He seemed to be able to sense what the Ken-cows were about to do before they knew themselves. Not one of his charges ever strayed or was lost. He even managed to discover several refugees that had escaped from 'steads the Ronin had destroyed and were wandering homeless about the valley. Misako was a natural weaver, capable of a delicacy matching that of the tiny water lizard that wove its nest among the reeds at the edge of the river. Obie seemed able to do most anything, though his forte was caring for the garden. Jerome found him several times, sitting and talking to the various vegetables, weeding and caring for them as if they were sentient. The garden's yields were truly amazing.

Chaka was the smiling, scoffing, good-humored leader of the whole gang. Her calmness and laughter filled the meadow with a joyful light Jerome could feel but never see. There was no question the 'stead was the most pleasant in the valley to visit. The fare was simple, the work hard, and the company always congenial.

The only thing that bothered Jerome was Chaka's constantly mocking attitude toward him. Once, when he had tried seriously to explain the reason for his wandering, she had laughed in his face and called him a silly fool. "You wander all over, looking under the rocks in your mind, for something that's standing right there in plain sight. Stop looking if you want to find it," she had chided him.

He had been annoyed by her attitude, especially since what she had said sounded just like something the Master would say. What right does a mere girl have to sound like a Master? he grumbled to himself. But a small part of his mind replied, This is no mere girl. This one walked away from the Sisterhood. This one seems to know more about the Mushin than you do.

Finally, one evening after having spent the day breaking ground for an extension of Obie's garden, Jerome decided to ask Chaka about her experiences at the Sisterhood. The girl shrugged and smiled. "I got tired of all the silliness and decided to leave."

"But why did you go at all, then?"

"I was Called. Dad said it would be best if I went. Besides, he said a few years in the Sisterhood would teach me a lot about the Mushin and Man's problem here on Kensho. It also showed me how absurd the whole Way of Passivity is."

Jerome's eyes opened wide. "What? The Passivity, absurd?"

She smiled smugly. "Sure."

"Explain," he requested.

Chaka sighed. "At times I wonder how you ever managed to leave the 'hood, much less how you've managed to survive since then. You're so dumb sometimes!

"Look, you know the Litany of the Way as well as I do. 'Being Causes Desiring. Desiring gives rise to Action. Action leads to Frustration. Frustration ignites Anger. Anger draws the Mushin. And the Mushin bring down the Madness'. That's what the Grandfathers taught us. And they gave us the Way of Passivity as a method for controlling the middle terms of this equation so we could avoid the inevitable movement from Being to Madness. The Way, with its Spiritual Exercises and Physical Disciplines, teaches us to control our Desire, to enclose it behind an iron wall of rigid passivity or Non-Action. Thus the chain is broken at its start and life on Kensho is possible."

Chaka laughed and shook her head. "It all seems so logical, so precise, so correct. It all came from the mind of Admiral Nakamura, they told us, so how could we question it? And it seems to work, at least to a degree.

"But think for a moment. The Grandfathers tell you to control your Desire, right? Well, then, what about controlling the Desire to control your Desire? Isn't that a Desire just like any other? Don't look so surprised," the girl chuckled. "You can see the possibilities of that, eh?"

"I think so," Jerome replied thoughtfully. "Once you Desire to control your Desire, you must take Action to accomplish it. Which leads to Frustration. Which leads to . . . Gods! I just thought of something else! Once you Desire to control your Desire, you've got to go on and Desire to control your Desire to control your Desire! And then . ."

Chaka held up her hands to stop Jerome. "Yes, yes, it recedes like that forever. That's the central contradiction in the Way of Passivity. What it all comes down to is that the Passivity doesn't really do away with Desire. It suppresses it, creating new Desire in a never-ending sequence. The Passivity keeps men chained to Desire rather than setting them free.

"But the worst of it is that the Passivity does something much more sinister. By bottling up our Desire, the Passivity actually creates a vast reservoir of Frustration and Anger. It literally makes us a perfect, constantly fruitful, emotional source for the Mushin! True, they can't gorge themselves like they did at First Touch, but enough emotional energy leaks out to keep the keen edge of their hunger satisfied.''

Jerome gaped incredulously at her. ''Gods,'' he whispered hoarsely, ''That means that the Brotherhoods and the Sisterhoods are really just . . .''

She nodded, finishing his thought for him. ''Just dining rooms for the Mushin. Since the Brothers and Sisters are those most proficient in the Way, they're a constant source of food for the Mushin. Which explains why there are so many Mushin all over every 'hood.''

The young man sat in stunned silence, his shoulders slumped, his glazed eyes staring blankly at the floor of the cabin. ''Gods,'' he muttered. ''Gods!'' When he looked up, there was a new light in his eyes. Softly he asked, ''And those who are Called?''

''The best. The ones who might figure it out if they had the time and opportunity. But once brought into the 'hoods and trained into the Way, the chance that they'll ever find the Truth is minimal. Those who pose no threat are left on the 'steads to breed.''

''And the Ronin?''

She tilted her head to one side, quizzically. ''That's one I don't quite understand myself. Obviously, they serve as a way of creating emotional food for the Mushin. All that killing means an orgiastic banquet for the mind leeches that come with the Ronin. But given the existence of the 'hoods, that hardly seems necessary.

"Of course, they could also act as a population control mechanism," she mused. "Sort of a culling force that keeps the human population down to a certain level. But why? You'd think that the more of us there were, the more emotions we'd generate and the more food the Mushin would have. It doesn't make sense to limit our numbers. We haven't even begun to exhaust the resources of the valleys. It can't be a question of future conservation when there's a whole empty planet. And this area alone could support a much larger population indefinitely. No," she shook her head, "no, I don't completely understand the function of the Ronin."

Jerome had no answer to offer. Idly fingering his Smoothstone, he stared absently at the floor, his mind absorbing this new information. He was beginning to realize just how little he really knew.

As the months continued to pass, Jerome felt a growing sense of frustration and dissatisfaction. It was not unlike the feeling he had experienced once before when the Master had promised to teach him the Way of the Sword and then had simply left him to sweep and cook for months on end. But this time it was not directed outward at another. Now it was directed inward with himself as the focus.

Uncomfortably, he acknowledged that two years had passed since he had left the Master and set off on his own to find the Way. His wandering, non-involved life-style had provided plenty of freedom and time to look within for the answer to

Nakamura's Koan and the key to the Way that would free all men on Kensho. The results, he admitted, had been nil. All the sitting, all the meditation, all the internal searching had yielded nothing. He was not one step closer to setting foot on the Way than he had been when he came down off the Mountain. In fact, he reminded himself, he had never even had another Satori experience, another awakening to the Truth, to equal either the one he had felt on the Mountain, or even the one he had undergone after killing the Grandfather.

Now, though, he was determined to succeed. He had climbed to an isolated spot on the valley's rim to be utterly alone. His vantage point was situated on the eastern edge of the valley, at a point where the mountains jutted sharply westward. Spread out below him, as far as his eyes could see, were the meadows, the forests, and the occasional farmsteads he had passed through. Here and there, he could catch a shining glimpse of the River, winding its way northward toward the Big Water.

Picking a spot with care, he sat down and began to arrange the contents of his pack around him. Within easy reach of his right hand, he placed a pitcher filled with water and a water skin from which he could refill it two more times. Opposite the water, close by his left hand, he set down a block of dried Ken-cow meat and a cake made of a mixture of crushed and dried fruits and vegetables. There was enough to last for several days if he ate sparingly.

His physical environment in order, he crossed

his legs and arranged his robe so that it was loose and non-constricting. Rocking gently back and forth, he found a balanced, restful posture for his body, and folded his hands in his lap. He was facing due north, so that the sun rose to his right and set to his left.

I will not move from this place until I find what I am looking for, he declared to himself and to the Universe at large. If necessary, I will die here.

When Jerome failed to show up for several days, Chaka began to worry. He had promised to stop by and help them slaughter and dress a couple of Ken-cows. Although she constantly teased the young man about being too serious and out of touch with reality, Chaka knew he had a strong sense of obligation and seldom failed to do as he promised. In addition, she admitted to herself, she rather missed the talks they had, for Jerome had an eager and incisive mind, even if he was a little stubborn and thick-skulled at times.

She sent Obie out to make the rounds of the nearby 'steads to see if there was any news of Jerome's whereabouts. It turned out that the Millers, further to the south by several 'steads, had been the last to see him, some five days previously. He had worked there for three days. Then, his sack stuffed with food and his waterskin brimming full, he had left. Their last view of him had been as he turned to wave just before entering the forest. He was heading south toward the valley wall.

Two more days passed, and with them came

rumors that a band of Ronin had entered the southern end of the valley, burning a 'stead just built by a young couple from the north. Both had managed to escape, since they were out in the forest gathering wood when the killers rushed the cabin. Hearing the cries of the attacking Ronin, they had fled through the trees.

Chaka decided to go and find Jerome. Something deep inside her realized it was time for the young wanderer to abandon his monastic aloofness. He must be brought into full contact with the reality of life—and death—in the valley. She sighed. It would be like pulling a Ken-wolf from its prey. Or better yet, like ripping a baby from its womb. But unless the baby abandoned its place of warmth and security, the man could never be. And this man *must* be.

Instinctively, Chaka understood that Jerome had a role to play in the scheme of things. Up to now, the young man had vaguely sensed the general direction he had to follow. But it was clear that he failed to comprehend precisely the part he was to fulfill. His ego, his personal goals and desires, clouded his vision, causing him to wander far from the correct path.

It wasn't that he didn't try. Indeed, all Jerome's energy was directed to answering Nakamura's Koan, to solving the mystery of the Way to freedom. The problem was rather the method he'd adopted to fulfill his mission. Jerome had rejected the traditional approach, the Way of Passivity, for good and substantial reasons. What the Grandfathers taught was rubbish, as Chaka herself had discovered. It had nothing to do with freedom from the Mushin or the Way mentioned in the Koan.

Jerome had replaced the Passivity with a furiously active seeking, first through the medium of the Way of the Sword, and now within himself. But all his activity was getting him nowhere, as Chaka had seen for herself. His struggle was valiant and courageous, to be sure. Yet the girl could not help but think of him as a swimmer doggedly breasting a strong current to reach safety while all he had to do was relax and move with the flow to attain the shore.

The crux of the matter lay in the fact that Jerome believed that the goals he so ardently sought were real, fixed objects capable of attainment and possession. But Chaka knew, in a way that goes beyond knowing, that the Self and the things it desired were mere illusions. They were the creations of an ego-distorted world view. For the girl understood that perception is a question of perspective. What seemed so immutable and essential to the young Seeker would disappear if he simply shifted his viewpoint.

A broader view of things had shown her that the idea of a world filled with static, fixed forms was nothing but the self-delusion of an unseeing eye. The truth was that the Universe was a fluid, ever-changing cosmos in which every object was constantly in the process of being created or destroyed or mutated into its opposite. The Self, the ego, was like a bubble in the River, a fleeting moment within the flow, shaped and formed by that which surrounded it, returning to it in a swirl of thoughtless annihilation.

That didn't mean one should run away to a mountain top, renouncing the world of sense perception and seeking the "real" aspect of all things in some transcendental Beyond. The real aspect *was* all things. The problem was not in accepting objects as real. They were real. But they were not separate, independent things or substances or entities. Rather, objects were processes or events. One could participate in them, but one could not possess them. If you tried to cling to them, they slipped through your fingers like water, leaving only frustration, pain, and suffering behind. As Chaka had learned, the only thing to do was to accept, even welcome, the fluidity and impermanence of the world and to immerse one's Self in it, moving with the flow.

This was Action in its truest sense. To the ego, it might seem very like the sort of forced Non-Action advocated by the Way of Passivity. But the Non-Action of True Action had nothing to do with the Passivity taught by the Grandfathers. Non-Action did not mean doing nothing and keeping silent. The stillness in stillness is not the real stillness. Since the Universe is never quiescent, never static, the only True Action must be stillness within movement. If one's Self is still, if one moves with the flow instead of struggling against it, what seems like Passivity or Non-Action to the grasping ego is just the opposite. For True Action means letting the world and the forces within it act for you. In this manner, everything can be done because *everything does itself*. Living naturally and spontaneously, the ego dissolves and the desire of the Self to divide the world into categories to be manipulated for personal satisfaction disappears. By letting go and letting be, one truly holds and fully is.

Somehow, Chaka had to make Jerome understand that his actions, tied as they were to his own individual desires and personal goals, were doomed to failure. The Seeker of the Way must cease *his* seeking before the real search could even begin. The only way to realize his quest was to abandon it. The girl didn't know how to go about convincing Jerome of this. But she did see that the first step was to somehow force him to return to the valley and take up the task only he could perform.

Giving the children specific instructions on what to do and how to hide in case of an emergency, she left one morning in search of Jerome.

The young man turned glazed eyes outward to focus on the creature that squatted in front of him. It was a girl. With dark hair and bright blue eyes. She was laughing.

"Why are you laughing," he managed to croak out. He had gone beyond hunger and thirst. Even his tiredness only came now when he opened his eyes.

"I'm laughing at the fool who comes to the top of the mountain to begin, when even the mountain begins in the valley."

He blinked at the girl. Then he closed his eyes again. She was doubtless just another one of his visions. There had been so many. Nakamura himself had come, singing his Koan in rhythmical cadence. The Master, too. The old man had threatened to hit Jerome with a boulder, but had snorted in derision when Jerome had tried to tell him to stop. "Words!" he had said scornfully and disappeared. Ribaud showed up and did a kata on the top of a grain of sand. Even the Grandfather's head had blown by, muttering incantations about swords and minds and meaning.

And now this girl. Familiar. He opened his eyes again. Strange. It was dark now. The sun was gone and one of Kensho's moons owned the sky. The girl was still there. Strange again. Most of his visitors departed.

The girl. Chaka. She pointed at the moon. "Do you see the moon?"

He nodded.

She held the finger she had pointed with before his eyes. "This is the pointing finger. It showed you the moon. Yet it is not the moon. Where is the moon?"

He nodded his head toward the shining orb that hung in the sky.

"When the finger has shown you the moon, you no longer pay attention to the finger. You pay attention to the moon. The finger only serves to point."

Jerome nodded again. This seemed right.

"The Master has shown you the Moon."

Again, this seemed to be the case. He acknowledged her statement.

"Then why do you persist in looking at his finger?"

The question shocked him to full alertness. "What do you mean?" he whispered, on the edge of understanding.

"The word is not the meaning. To speak of fire does not burn the mouth. The word ice does not freeze the tongue.

"The traveling is not the Way."

Straining, his mind tried to leave him behind. I see . . . almost . . . almost . . . I see . . . ran the thoughts, trying to escape the grooves he had forced them into. Almost. Almost. And then it failed him and the dawning light dimmed and he was on the side of the mountain at night with Chaka squatting before him, her face filled with hope that died as she saw the glow fade from his eyes.

He looked down, confused, embarrassed, mortified. "I . . . I . . . don't understand," he whispered in defeat.

Sadly, Chaka reached out and took his hand. "You aren't supposed to 'understand.' You're supposed to know."

Jerome mumbled a reply. Then he looked up, gloom written over his features. "I came here to find the Way, the answer to the Koan, or die trying. I failed. I can't find the Way and I can't die."

"You're still looking at the finger. You're trying to will the Way. But where there is a Will, there is no Way."

"Jerome, while you are up here trying to solve the Koan or die trying, there are men, women, and children down in that valley who are really dying. In agony."

His head lifted wearily. "The Ronin are back?"
She nodded.

Helplessly, he looked about. "What can I do? I search and I search to find a Way to free all men. And I find nothing but hunger and visions."

Gently she lifted the hand she held until it was level with his eyes. "That hand can hold a sword. That mind can fight without losing control. The Master has shown you the Way to do those things. You can fight the Ronin. You can save those lives."

"But that is not the Way," he protested. "That's merely involvement in the world all over again. It might serve for a while to help, but it wouldn't solve the real problem. The Ronin are just a symptom. The Mushin are the enemy. Until we are free of the Mushin, everything else is irrevelant." Fiercely, he gritted out, "I must find the Way! Nothing else can help!"

She dropped his hand and picked up the water pitcher he had placed near him. It was empty. Chaka poured some water into it from her water skin. She handed it to Jerome. "Before you drink, look into the pitcher and tell me if it is half-empty or half-full."

Suddenly realizing the full force of his thirst, he grabbed the pitcher. Controlling his desire to drink, he followed her command, looking inside. It was half-full. He made to answer her and then suddenly realized that if it was half-full, it was also half-empty. Which you called it depended on your own choice. But she had asked him to call it one or the other before he drank. For several more moments he stared at the water, unable to decide if the pitcher was more accurately described as half-full or half-empty.

Chaka's hand darted forth and grabbed the pitcher from him. With a quick movement she poured the contents over his head. Then, laughing at his surprised sputtering, she smashed the pitcher on the rock. "While you dither over words," she said, "the water is gone. Your thirst was not enough to force you beyond the particular. Is your desire for the Way stronger than your thirst?"

"But my thirst is personal. My wish to find the Way is for all Men," he protested.

"Words," she snapped her fingers. "The fact is, *you* choose to search for the Way. And while you search, others die.

"Compassion, Jerome. Compassion is what you lack. You are so high, so mighty, so pure. Gods, you've lived virtually your whole life in the 'hood! What do you know of the suffering of others? Everything you've done has been for your own reasons, even your desire to save the race is to further your own need for revenge!

"I've watched you and listened to you for over a year now. You're a good man, but you still look at the finger, not at the moon. Come down off the Mountain, now and forever. One old Master sitting alone on the slopes is enough. And even his example you ignore. Didn't you tell Tommy about the way he killed the Ronin band?

"You're needed, Jerome. Now. In the valley, not on the Mountain. Come down."

"You don't understand," he cried, his voice despairing.

"No," she replied. "But I know." Chaka stood and looked down at Jerome. "Gaylor needs the door to his cabin reinforced. With the Ronin showing up again, it better be done soon." With that she turned and left.

Mourning his failure, Jerome sat and watched the other three moons rise. With the coming of the dawn, he rose weakly and left.

Chapter XI

DESPONDENT OVER HIS failure to make the final breakthrough to the Way, Jerome wandered aimlessly about the mountainous rim of the valley for several days. His mind and body still in a turmoil after the recent experience, he mulled over his predicament.

The things Chaka said had moved him profoundly. The fact was, he *could* fight the Ronin, he *could* save the lives of the 'steaders. But equally true was the fact that such an action was not a final solution to the problem. It treated the symptoms, not the disease, dealt with the particular, not the general.

That was actually the most confusing aspect of the paradox Chaka had created in his mind. To save the 'steaders, he had to find the Way. Which meant he had to withdraw, meditate, and take no part in the trivia of daily existence. But to save the 'steaders, he had to fight and become involved, functioning wholly within the world of daily happenings. To do one, he had to give up the other. But neither alone made any sense.

Around and around his mind went, oscillating between two seemingly irreconcilable choices. He realized Chaka wanted him to carry what the Master had called the Sword of Life and fight against the Sword of Death. But if he held the Sword of Life, how would he ever have the time to pursue the other Sword, the Sword of No Sword which the Master had enjoined him to seek?

Finally, no nearer a solution than when he had started, Jerome returned to the valley. At first he stayed away from Chaka and the children. He wasn't ready to face them in his defeat. So, resuming his old pattern, he moved from 'stead to 'stead, but kept mainly to the upper reaches of the valley, far south of the old Chien place. There was no danger from the Ronin, since they had departed the valley after burning two cabins.

Eventually, he found himself drifting unconsciously northward. And in about a month, the day came when he stood once more at the edge of the clearing, his heart soaring with joy as Tommy ran, yelling greetings, to leap into his arms and Chaka came to the door of the cabin to wave.

The evening was a warm one. After dinner the five of them went and sat on the banks of the River, looking up at the moons and stars. The silence between and around them was relaxed and natural.

"Chaka," Jerome's voice was like a pebble striking the smooth surface of a pool, sending rings of meaning outward. "Chaka, I've been thinking about what you said up there. About me and the Ronin, I mean."

The girl just nodded, her face in shadow.

"I . . . well, I'm confused," the young man continued. "Oh, I don't mean that I didn't understand what you said. What I mean is, well . . .

"Look, Chaka, I don't think you really know how important it is for me to find the Way. I . . . I wasn't Called, you know. I didn't leave my home to go to the Brotherhood. The Ronin forced me out, ripped me out. They killed my parents. Burned the 'stead. I survived, like Tommy, and the Fathers found me.

"The Brotherhood's all I've ever known, really. Like you said. But there is one other thing I've known, deeply. That's the need to strike back at the Mushin for what they did. Not only what they did to me, but what they do to all men. I sensed, don't ask me how, I just did, that the Passivity is the wrong way to fight the Mushin. It isn't what Nakamura meant, no matter what anybody says. And so I decided to try and find the Way the Koan really talked about.

"The Sword had played such an important part in my life, I guess I just naturally gravitated toward it. And the Way of the Sword seemed like a good candidate for Nakamura's Way. After all, it seemed to stress Action rather than Passivity and . . . well, anyway, I decided to follow it.

"So I asked for a Personal Audience with the Grandfather to request permission to go up the Mountain and study the Way of the Sword with the Old Master." For a moment, the silence of the night filled Jerome's mind, replacing the words. He hesitated for just a breath or two, wondering how much he should tell. Then he decided that Chaka was probably the only other human on Kensho he could share his secret with and be sure of a sympathetic reception. After all, the girl had run away from the Sisterhood herself.

He took a deep breath and continued. "I . . . I went to the Grandfather's cell. And I made my request. It . . . it was a long time before he answered. When he did, it was with a chant." His breath came more quickly as he remembered that experience, the creeping tentacles of meaning seeping and twisting through his mind, over and around and through his controls. He shuddered.

"The . . . the Grandfather tried to take over my mind." He could hear Chaka's soft exclamation. "No, I'm not imagining things. The Grandfather did things to my mind. Things like the Mushin do. I . . . I . . . I suddenly saw some sort of connection between them. And I reacted. I killed him."

Chaka was sitting up rigidly now, leaning toward Jerome, her shadowed face alight with interest. "Killed him? How?" she asked.

"Well, I struck him with the side of my hand. His head flew off."

"And?" she prompted tensely.

"I passed out. But when I woke up again, I went and looked at him. Chaka, he was hollow! Empty!

A shell! I had a vision then. I saw my journey spread out before me. The Mountain was there, and the Master. And beyond that. It went beyond. But it's all fuzzy now."

The girl touched his arm. "Hollow?" she asked, her voice tight with excitement. "You said 'hollow'?"

Jerome nodded. "Empty. Nothing inside."

"Then what makes you think he was alive?"

The young man blinked. "What? What do you mean?"

"You said you 'killed' the Grandfather, but that there was nothing there except an empty shell. How can you kill an 'empty shell'? How do you know the Grandfather was anything more than a hollow shell? How do you know he was alive at all?"

"But he talked to me!" Jerome protested.

"You said he invaded your mind. Did he talk, or did he directly invade your mind the way the Mushin do?" Her eyes glittered with interest.

"He . . . he talked, I think," Jerome responded uncertainly. "Or maybe not. After all, I couldn't see his lips move. It was too dark."

Chaka laughed. "They don't have lips, silly! Only a mouth slit. Look, Jerome, this is very important. Don't you see? You said the Grandfather could do things like the Mushin do. Things with your mind. You saw a connection between the two." He nodded with enthusiasm.

"Yes, a connection. I still think there's a connection."

"It makes all the sense in the world," Chaka

continued excitedly. "The Grandfathers bring us the Way of Passivity which makes us perfect cattle for the Mushin! The Grandfathers Call our best into the 'hoods where they can feed the mind leeches. The Grandfathers set up rules and regulations to keep things in this nice, tidy arrangement for generations."

Jerome struck his forehead in amazement. "Gods, yes! Why didn't I think of that! But . . . but . . . if that's true, then the Grandfathers are as much creatures of the Mushin as the Ronin are!"

For a long moment they sat in mutual stunned silence. Finally, the girl nodded slowly. "Yes, yes it's possible."

The young man shook his head from side to side as if trying to shake an idea loose. "There's so much I don't know. And so many possibilities."

Chaka made a decision. "Jerome," she said, her voice firm. "I think it's time I told you about Dad's secret. It'll add another piece to the puzzle. The more you know the better. Maybe between the two of us, we can figure it all out. Or at least enough of it to understand what's going on."

He nodded agreement. "Gods, yes! I feel like I'm walking in the dark at the edge of a chasm. Anything that will shed a little more light would be welcome. But what do you mean, Rudy's secret?"

"You only knew him as an old 'steader, Jerome. But he was much more than a simple old man. He entered a 'hood way down on the Plain when he was only ten. Ten and Called! Imagine. He left at fifteen. Just walked out one day and spent the next several years wandering all over the area we inhabit on Kensho. Dad knew more than any man or woman about the Mushin, the Ronin, and our human settlement. He drew a map, you know. No, I don't have it. I looked, but he must have taken it with him when he left. I saw it though, just before I left for the 'hood. He showed it to me and explained the whole thing very carefully. I didn't understand why at the time, but now I do.''

''Humanity lives in a very restricted area, Jerome. To the east is the Sea and no one's ever even tried to cross it as far as I know. Mountains surround us on the west and north and part of the south. The rest of the area to the south is covered by the Great Swamp. It runs right into the Sea at the place where the Waters join it. It'd be suicide to try to penetrate that muck hole.

''So we live in a cup, held against the Sea by the mountains and the bottomless slime of the swamp. A nice, limited little enclave. A big pen for the emotional cattle.''

''How do you know it's a pen?'' he asked.

''Because there are openings. And I know that because I've seen them with my own eyes. Dad took me there years ago. There are passes through the mountains, one at the head of this very valley. And on the other side of the passes is a vastness that goes on and on forever. There's enough room there for millions and millions of us, space enough to fulfill the purpose of the Pilgrimage twenty times over!''

Excited, Jerome grabbed her hands. ''But . . . but if that's all there, if there's a way out of here, a way to escape, why haven't we found it yet? Why don't we all just go?''

Calmly, Chaka replied. ''I said it was a pen.

There are exits. But they're closed."

The young man stared. "Closed," he wondered aloud, "closed by what, by whom?"

"I think it's best if you see for yourself. We'll leave tomorrow." With that, Chaka rose, gathered up the children, and walked across the meadow to the cabin.

Jerome stayed in the moonslight, idly tossing his Smoothstone from hand to hand, deep in abstracted thought over the new ideas that crowded his mind.

The next morning, Chaka and Jerome took provisions and, giving careful but probably unnecessary instructions to the children, set off up the valley. For two days, they followed the ever-narrowing valley southward. The River became a mere stream, tumbling wildly over a rough terrain that became more chasm-like with every twist. Eventually it died in a small, deep lake nestled in a broad cup surrounded by mountains. They were forced to take to the mountains themselves.

Even then, there was a trail of sorts. It wound around, up and down, in and out. But it was clear that something or someone passed this way fairly regularly. Jerome was puzzled by this since he couldn't image any way to farm the rocky soil. 'Steaders simply couldn't make a living among the mountains.

Soon, at a point where the trail entered a narrow defile in the rocks, Chaka turned off and struck out across the virgin slopes. When Jerome questioned her, she replied shortly, "This way we can approach unseen." But unseen by whom or what was not discussed.

The late afternoon of the third day brought them to a point where they could travel no farther. They stood at the crest of a small ridge, the reverse side of which dropped vertically into a deep chasm. Further to the west, they could see the mountains falling away until they merged with a distant plain.

Awed by the sight of so much immensity, Jerome stood spellbound. Though she had seen it before, the girl too was silenced by the grandeur of the vista. Finally the young man found his voice and said softly, "It goes on forever."

Chaka echoed, "Forever. It's what our people were promised when we came here. It's what the Pilgrimage is all about."

Excitement replacing his awe, Jerome turned, grabbing her hands. "Chaka, do you think the Mushin are there? Do you think we could be free, rid of them and the Madness if we went out there? Could we escape?"

She shrugged. "Who knows? They might be there, might not."

He rushed on. "But it would be worth trying, wouldn't it? Worth taking a chance to get all that?" He gestured toward the purple horizon.

"Sure," she replied, "except for one thing."

"What's that?" he asked. "Surely it can be overcome!"

Chaka snorted. "Yeh. Surely. Come on. I'll show you the problem over this way. Not more than a couple minutes walk along the slope in that direction. But go carefully and control your mind."

Startled, he fell in behind her. "My mind? What

does my mind have to do with it?''

Over her shoulder she whispered, ''Quiet! Pretend like you're in the 'hood!''

Silently, calming his mind with the Litany, he followed her down the ridge, up another slope, through a boulder-strewn gulley, up a shattered rocky face to a broad ledge that jutted into space. From where he stood behind the girl, he could not see what lay beneath the ledge. Chaka motioned him to his hands and knees. Quietly he crawled to her side.

Leaning close she whispered in his ear, ''Feel 'em? Reach out just a little with your mind.''

Carefully Jerome extended his awareness. In a flash, he felt the tingling, burning sensation that meant Mushin were in the area. His eyes wide with surprise, he turned back to the girl. She nodded affirmation and gestured toward the edge of the ledge.

''Crawl up to the rim, slowly and quietly. Keep your mind calm as a pool on a still night. The place is filthy with Mushin. When you get to the edge, peek over carefully. Show as little of your head as possible. It's maybe 150 feet to the bottom, so you'll be able to see everything. That is if the light holds. Go, then come back.''

Moving as gently and silently as he knew how, Jerome approached the edge. Reaching it, he lay flat and slowly pushed his head out until his eyes cleared the rock rim of the ledge and he could look downward.

He was overlooking a twisting valley. The floor

was no more than 200 yards wide in most places, but was flat and lightly grassed. Scattered here and there were lump-like mounds of rock. A slight movement over to his left revealed what looked like a runty Ken-cow grazing on the grass.

Suddenly, he started and stared harder. Something had just come out of one of the mounds! A man! Fearing discovery, he pulled his head back and retreated as swiftly as possible to where Chaka waited.

"Men," he whispered intensely when he reached her side, "there are men down there!"

"Not men," she corrected. "Ronin. Lots of them. Maybe fifty or more. Both male and female. That explains the Mushin."

A haunted look flitted like a shadow behind her eyes. "And then there are the others," she muttered, barely audible.

"Others?" Jerome queried.

"The Burnt-Out Ones."

He simply stared.

She continued, almost as if speaking to herself. "Dad knew what they were. He'd seen it happen. Burning Out. I've never seen it and I guess I'm glad. The Mushin do it once in a while to a Ronin when he starts getting too slow. Sometimes they just let him die and feed on him. But sometimes they burn him out. Destroy his mind. Not kill him. Just burn out his mind so he's a walking zombie.

"You see, Jerome, Mushin can't *do* anything. They can't swing their own swords, so to speak. So they get men to do it for them. But a man has a mind of his own, even a Ronin. And while they can sort of steer the mind, the Mushin can't completely control it.

"But a Burnt-Out mind is different. There's no will left. No emotions. The Mushin can give instructions and the body will react. Clumsily, badly, but it will work. Those huts, for example, were built out of rocks by Burnt-Out Ones.

"And Burnt-Out Ones can breed, too." She shuddered at the thought. "They can create new little Ronin." A grim smile played over her lips. "Apparently it's easier to make a little Ronin, bring him up wrong, and train him to do worse, than it is to take an ordinary kid and ruin him. Of course, ordinary people still go Ronin, though it seems to happen less often with each generation, but the Mushin make sure of the supply with the Burnt-Out Ones. Ronin usually don't last long. Especially the women. So a constant supply is a problem."

Jerome felt sick. "Gods," he mumbled. "The poor devils."

"Yeh," the girl nodded. "Now you know where the Ronin come from, in both senses of the word. There are probably other places like this. Dad said he'd found one way up north in the mountains the other side of the Valley.

"And now you know what I meant when I said there was a problem in getting through to that plain we saw."

Jerome frowned. "I don't see what you're driving at."

"No? Well, what do you think you were just looking at?"

"A valley," he replied. "It was a narrow, little valley in the mountains."

"Silly," she scoffed. "that's not just a valley. It's a pass! It's one of those ways out of the pen I told you about."

Surprised, he sat upright. "Pass?" he hissed in question. "You mean that valley leads through the mountains to the other side?"

Chaka nodded affirmatively. "Dad said so. I've never checked myself, but I'll take his word for it. That valley," she gestured with her thumb, "is a way out, an escape hatch. It's the gateway to the plains and endless room."

Jerome sank back to the ground again, resting on one elbow. "But it's blocked. By the Ronin, And the Mushin."

"Blocked," the girl agreed. "Like a stopper in a jug."

"And any poor 'steaders who might have found the way . . ."

She finished the sentence for him by drawing her forefinger across her throat.

"But why?" he asked no one in particular. "Why don't they want us to expand? Surely they could follow us. Some might escape, but they'd end up with a greater supply of food than ever! It makes no sense! They have everything to gain from there being more of us."

Shrugging her own inability to answer the question, the girl began to move back away from the ledge and the Ronin-filled pass. Mumbling his confusion, Jerome followed.

They made a cold and silent camp that night,

chewing moodily on pieces of dried Ken-cow flesh. The moons which rose and fled across the sky, the moons which seemed so warm and full of meaning when watched from down in the valley, here seemed dead and frigid, empty of purpose.

When they arose the next morning, it was to a day that promised rain. Moving swiftly, with a sense of urgency coming both from their desire to avoid a chilly wetting and to leave the loathsome Ronin camp behind, they reached the well-worn mountain trail in the afternoon.

As they stepped onto the path, Chaka gave a gasp of surprise and immediately dropped to her knees. "Look," she whispered intensely, "fresh tracks!" Jerome knelt beside her. The footprints were clear. His eye traveled to a small pebble that had been pushed from its resting place by a careless foot. The spot where it had been was still moist. He looked at Chaka. She nodded. "This morning. Only a few hours at the most. I make it out to be about nine or ten of them."

Ronin! The raiders were returning to the valley. And in force! He doubted they would stay in one band: more likely they would split in two or even three smaller groups. Less internal tension that way. Also, they could cover more territory without running into each other. But that many descending on the valley at one time meant disaster for many 'steaders!

The two of them stood. Chaka faced him, her hands on her hips, anger in her eyes and plainly written on her face. "The biggest raid ever! And you'll sit by and do nothing?"

Jerome would not meet her gaze. "Look at me, Jerome!" He raised his eyes uncertainly to find the full glare of her gaze boring into him. Frightened and fascinated by the very intensity, he found himself unable to break away now that contact had been made.

Scorn was heavy in her voice: "You're like a herdboy riding a Ken-cow in search of a Ken-cow. You search for the Way. But you can't find the Way by looking for it. It isn't here. It isn't there. You struggle with all your energy to resolve contradictions, to choose between alternatives. Around and around you go, yet the only thing you're chasing is your own tail."

"But I must struggle!" he interrupted with a cry. "I must try! I've dedicated my whole life to my search. I can't give it up now!" The cry came from his soul, wrenched from the very center of his being by the agony of his indecision.

"Your life!" she laughed harshly. "There is no 'your life'. There is only Life. You look out of your eyes and you think you see the world. Then you try to act on it, forcing it to change and yield as you see fit, trying to make it conform to your own idea of what it should be.

"But it's not there. Not as a separate realm filled with things you can form and shape and bend to your will. Life is an interconnected whole, a single piece of cloth. The same threads that create one thing, weave the pattern that forms all the others. They only have meaning and being in their twining together as they mutually unfold the warp and woof of the entire Universe.

"The only way to act is not to act. Place your Self selflessly in the flow of Life. Let a compassionate sensitivity to everything around you be your guide. Don't try to cling to 'things.' Interact with the process of their being, participate in their doing of themselves. Don't pick and choose and discriminate. Live naturally and spontaneously. Eat when you're hungry. Sleep when you're tired.

"And fight when you are threatened!"

The words hit Jerome with tremendous force. In them, he heard many echoes of what the Master had said, things he had not understood at the time, but which had remained in his mind like stones thrown into a pool of muddy water. Now he could almost see them, even though the water was still cloudy and turbulent. He had the feeling that if only he could reach out and calm the water, force it to become clear, he would discover some message of great importance.

For a timeless time he stood there, not moving, not reaching out to still the water. The pressure in his mind was almost unbearable. Choices spilled across his awareness like lightning across a dark sky. Confusion fell in torrents, drowning decision in swirling emptiness.

He suddenly realized his eyes were closed. Opening them, he looked outward. Lightning daggered the clouds. Rain sprawled across the ground in hopeless abandon. Thunder crashed against the sky and tumbled down to fill the emptiness around him.

He stood alone.

Chapter XII

JEROME PANICKED. He fled headlong down the trail, through the rain. "Chaka!" he called out. "Chaka!" His mind was reeling. "Chaka! Chaka!" An overwhelming sense of horror and doom filled him. "Chaka!"

He ran, ever downwards, ever northwards, ever on the trail of Chaka and the Ronin. Among the trees, in the valley proper now, he sped, gasping for air. Suddenly he halted, baffled.

It cost him precious minutes, but the tracks told their story: the Ronin had split into two groups, one heading toward the western edge of the valley, the other staying close to the River.

And there, draped across a bush on the river bank, was a torn piece of cloth—Chaka's!

Winded now, he trotted, sucking in great gasps of wet air. The rain began to hestitate, but Jerome kept on, following the Ronin and Chaka. Occasionally the Ronin would leave the river for a while; ever and again, in an agony of frustration, he would have to double back to make sure of the trail.

Still, when dark finally came, he had covered an incredible distance. The penalty was legs that could no longer hold him up. He collapsed in a sodden heap and slept in the gentle drizzle that still fell.

Sleep, despite exhaustion, ended well before dawn. The new day was dark and cloudy, but at least no rain fell. He stood. The legs would hold. He could continue. But where was the girl? How could she have traveled so fast? Why hadn't he caught up?

Slowly at first, but gathering speed as he warmed up, Jerome went on. About noon, weak from hunger, he gathered some Ko pods and sipped some river water. The tracks were fresher now. He was closing the gap. In addition, this area was well known to him.

He shuddered. Yes, well known! The Ronin were heading directly for the farmstead where Tommy, Misako, and Obie waited!

Then he heard it, off to his left. The yipping of Ronin, the yowling of the killers closing on their prey!

The sound had frozen him into fearful immobility. Now the sudden understanding of what it meant galvanized him into instant action. Weariness fell away like old skin sloughed off by a tree lizard. He sprang ahead, his mind a fury of anguish. The Ronin weren't attacking the 'stead! They were attacking. . . . .! The thought was too much to consciously formulate and remain sane.

Even as he sped through the forest and across grassy meadows, a new sound joined the chorus of animal howlings. From the west came an echo! The second band of Ronin!

Full realization of what was happening hit him with such force he staggered beneath the blow. Crashing into a tree, he clung to the rough support for a moment, regaining his breath and his grip on sanity. Both bands, he thought. Of course, both bands! Then no hope, no hope.

The shrieking in the distance rose to a crescendo of surprise and outrage. Frightful squealings filled the forest air, riding like bloated spiders on the gentle breeze. The roaring hit a high, united climax and then separated into a few minor whimperings, rolling back like a retreating wave from a coast of tortured cliffs.

Jerome crumpled to the ground, head in hands. It's over, he mourned silently. Over. Then, in a sorrow deeper than any emotion he had ever felt, he rose and dragged himself on through the woods to where he knew boundless agony awaited.

Stepping over and around the bodies twisted in death, he approached the huddled form that lay in the center. Tears ran down his face and great sobs racked his body as he turned Chaka's body over and straightened her robe to cover the gaping wounds in her flesh.

He stroked the face, calm in death. The sparkle

and flash were gone, but strangely enough, the beauty remained. "Why?" he whispered to ears beyond hearing. "Why?"

But he knew. She had destroyed the Ronin menace. Acting as bait, she had attracted the first band, pulling them behind her in hot pursuit. Then she had run straight to the west, where she knew the other band stalked, seeking prey of its own. The maneuver had worked with ferocious precision. Both bands had spotted her and both had pursued. When they ran headlong into each other, their killing rage had been so inflamed that each had set upon and slaughtered the other. Only one or two had survived the clash, and they had probably slunk off into the woods to die of their wounds or to head back up into the mountains. The valley was safe. For now.

But Chaka had been caught between the two bands and was dead.

Bending down, he slid one arm beneath her shoulders, the other under her knees. He lifted the body with him as he stood. Hugging the slight form close, he began to walk through the woods toward the 'stead where the children awaited the homecoming of the adults.

As he walked, the numbness of the first shock began to wear off. Slowly, he began to comprehend the true size of the aching emptiness that Chaka's death created inside him. Amazed, he understood for the first time precisely how much the girl had meant to him.

Tears began to roll down his cheeks again and he felt himself drowning in grief. A tight feeling across his chest made it almost impossible to breathe. For a moment, it became too much to bear, and he stopped, sagging against a tree.

Gods, he thought, I loved you and didn't even know it! I was looking in every direction but the right one, trying to understand everything but the thing that mattered!

The pain in his gut became so real, so palpable, that he couldn't continue to stand. With a groan, he slid down the trunk to his knees, bending miserably over the still form.

Gone! his mind cried, lost in a vast anguish. Gone!

For long moments he knelt there, his mind a blank of despair. Then he heard the echo of a laugh winging weightless through the emptiness. A mere bubble of joy, it floated amid the boundless grief, tiny, unimportant, yet more potent than anything in the boundless universe of his mind.

It was Chaka's laugh. He recognized it, the warmth, the fullness, the slight teasing lilt of it.

Suddenly the bubble exploded and illuminated his mind with the glow of Chaka's mirth. It spread rapidly and Jerome could see clearly what he had never consciously noticed before. His love. Her love. Their love. And the meaning of it all.

Love, he realized, wasn't at all what he had thought it was. It wasn't desiring or even enjoying some "beloved" person or thing or idea. Love wasn't clinging to something or clutching it to your bosom. It wasn't possession.

Love was participation, interaction, process: flow and movement between two objects themselves in constant change. It was a relationship that transformed itself as well as the objects it tied together. Like music or a waterfall it only existed and could only be enjoyed in motion; one couldn't capture it, enclose it, restrict it, preserve it. Only act it.

The greatest joy of all was to act it in full consciousness of that action. To be totally submerged in the process, to become one with it, to feel it all about you as it mutated and shifted, was the height of ecstasy. It was true fulfillment because it was continual, not momentary or static.

Such a love could never die. Things and persons and ideas, even the most important and desirable, passed away in the merest flicker of the eye. But movement and flow never ceased. A ripple started here, reverberated forever from every corner of existence. By pulling one small thread in the fabric of life, you caused the unravelling of whole sections of the cloth.

As the glow of Chaka's laugh had illuminated her love, now her love shone brightly on other things. Jerome saw that their love had spread far beyond the two of them, ever outward in growing ripples of relationship. The children, Tommy, Misako, and Obie, were there, interwoven into a web of action and meaning. He loved them all and they all loved him.

His awareness expanded even further, the light in his mind moving with it. He saw the network of interactions between himself and every 'steader in the valley. All of them, every one, was suffused with love. "Compassion" was the word Chaka had used. But it just meant love, love in its widest sense.

At last Jerome understood what the girl had meant when she had told him he lacked compassion. The flow and movement he now discerned had always been there, forever involving him with those around him. But he had been blind to it all. Instead of valuing it for what it was, he had attempted to use it, to manipulate it for his own ends. Everything, every relationship, had been subordinated to his quest for the Way.

And where was the Way? He didn't know. But he now realized it couldn't be found by doing what he had been doing. Chaka was right. Where there was Will, there was no Way: if one moved against the current, against his very nature, nothing but frustration could come of it.

Chaka, he admitted, had always moved with the current. It wasn't a conscious intention on her part. Rather, it was simply the girl's nature. Even her last act, her death, had been like that. She had immediately grasped the situation, seen what she must do, and had done it without hesitation.

She saw things I never saw, understood things I never understood, he confessed. Somehow, Chaka had viewed the world from a different perspective and had comprehended a larger landscape of meaning. Just like the Old Master, he realized. No, not exactly the same. The Master was an old man and had spent most of his lifetime achieving his present understanding. Chaka was a young girl and seemed to have come by it naturally. How could that be?

He shook his head in resignation. It didn't make any sense. Perhaps someday he would understand. But for the present, the most he could do was to try to accept.

Gradually, Jerome became conscious of the world around him once more. He looked down at the still face and smiled. You're not really gone, Chaka. The ripples you made in Reality will go right on influencing every little thing all of us do just as if you were still walking beside us. You'll always be with me. And with the children. And with the valley.

A tear ran through his smile. You've taught me what compassion really means, he thought. You are right. My Way can wait. I'll take up the sword and use what the Master has taught me.

I'll do what I can, he told her. I'll do what I can.

Tommy rubbed the tears off his cheeks, leaving dirt streaks behind. "We won't have to go away, will we, Jerome?" he asked, a tremor in his voice. "I don't want to go away from Obie and 'Sako." The older girl put her arm around his shoulder to comfort him.

Jerome smiled. "No, Tommy. We won't have to go away. I'm not as good a cook as Chaka, but I can learn. We'll stay together, right here. I'll have to be gone once in a while, but between the four of us, I imagine we'll make do."

Obie tried to smile, but it was too soon. With a stiff face he replied, "Good. Jerome, will you teach me how to handle a sword?"

Startled, Jerome, looked at the boy. "Sword?

Uhhh, I don't know. Why?"

"You'll need help," came the simple reply.

"Help?"

"Killing Ronin. That is what you're going to do, isn't it? That's why you'll be gone once in a while?" Obie asked.

Nodding, Jerome felt surprised at the child's perceptiveness. "Yes, I'll be killing Ronin. But I don't think a sword is quite the thing for someone your age. Hmmmmmmm, maybe I can think of something else."

Obie nodded grimly. "Something else would be fine if it will kill Ronin."

"Me too," Tommy whispered as they left the grave. "Me too."

Jerome stood in the meadow where the dead Ronin sprawled. Croaking carrion lizards flapped just above his head, angry at being disturbed while feeding. Twice now, he had carefully searched the area. They aren't here, he admitted. One of the Ronin must have come back and picked up the swords. Or perhaps another band had happened by, drawn by the circling lizards, and found the treasure trove of weapons.

So, he thought, it won't be a simple matter of picking up an abandoned sword. I'll have to earn it the hard way. Actually, the idea rather pleased him. There was a certain reluctance on his part to take a sword that might have helped to kill Chaka. He shuddered now at the thought. No, he realized, better that I get one from an opponent I've bested myself. It'll have more meaning.

The only question was how. One just didn't walk up to a Ronin and ask for a sword. Especially when one had only a simple knife for a weapon. He reached into his pocket. Feeling around, he found his Smoothstone and the knife he had brought with him so many years ago when he had left the Brotherhood. Taking it out, he looked it over. Mainly, he used it for eating, for cutting the tough meat of Ken-cows. But the blade was fairly long, five, six inches of good iron. He tested the edge with his thumb. Not very sharp, but that could be remedied.

It wasn't much, but a plan began to form in his mind. Humming, he left the meadow and entered the forest, searching for a way to transform an idea into reality.

It took him about an hour to find a suitable young ironwood sapling growing in the forest depths. It was straight and about three inches wide. By removing the bark and shaving it down, he created a staff about six feet in length—exactly as tall as he—and about two inches in diameter. Softly, slowly, he went through the motions of the kata forms he had learned so long ago in the Brotherhood while studying the Way of the Staff. Then he had been impatient with the careful, precise demands Father Chandrika had made on his students. Jerome had been anxious to move on to the sword, and had wanted to get through preliminary studies, one of which was the staff, as soon as possible. Now, he moved with a new appreciation of what Chandrika had been trying to bring out in his students. The movements of the staff were beautifully smooth and flowing, with many graceful circles and sweeping gestures.

Remembering what the Master had said about holding the sword, Jerome let go of the staff and instead of doing the kata, let the kata do him. For some time he simply moved about, gliding from place to place, weaving a dance in harmony with his surroundings. Yet every motion, every thrust, every swirl, was a death-dealing blow to an imaginary opponent, or a timely block and counter.

Finally, his mind joyful and relaxed by the effects of the dance, he stopped. Yes, he thought, this will do. Just one modification to the staff, a simple selection of certain techniques, the elimination of others, and he would be ready.

For two days, he worked on his weapon. First, he cut a notch in one end of the staff. Then he took the haft off his knife and inserted the blade in the notch. This was bound in place with careful, tight windings of cord made from Ken-cowgut. Then he coated the staff with tree sap. The sap dried, shrinking, to form a hard surface that held the blade firmly and strongly in place. The finishing touch was to sharpen both edges of the blade until he could cut a hair with either side.

A week of experimentation and practice passed as Jerome learned the balance, characteristics, advantages and drawbacks of his weapon. Since it was long, it could keep a swordsman, whose weapon had a much shorter reach, at bay. It wouldn't work forever against a really good opponent, of course, but it gave its wielder a fighting chance against any but a Master. One could thrust or slash with the blade, block with the shaft, and even deliver a tremendous blow with the blunt end. While the ironwood wouldn't be able to sustain a direct, full-power blow from a sharp sword, it was tough enough to survive glancing ones; blocking was more a matter of deflection than of stopping a blow.

Jerome realized that a larger blade would improve the attack value of the weapon, just as a shorter length would make it easier to maneuver for defense. A point on the unbladed end would be useful, too. Yet, all in all, the experiment was a successful one. Technique was more a matter of avoiding the opponent's blows and forcing him to commit himself than of direct attack. And circular motions were more efficient than rectilinear ones.

He let Obie try the new weapon several times, and was impressed when the boy's initial clumsiness rapidly gave way to a certain grace and understanding of the simple techniques for managing the blade and staff. Obie tended to be very conservative in his motions, making smaller circles, shorter movements. He kept the blade constantly in motion, weaving a wall of sharp death some four or five feet from his body. The thought occurred to Jerome that two or three people armed with such weapons would present a rather formidable foe, even to three or four Ronin. He mentioned the idea to Obie and then filed it away in his own mind for later action.

The day came when he felt he was ready. Taking some provisions, but leaving behind his medallion, his Smoothstone, and all his other personal belongings, he headed south toward the tip of the valley. Cautiously, he retraced the path he had gone over with Chaka. Every stone recalled memories of their trip together. Once more the girl walked beside him.

At the point where they had originally turned off the Ronin track, he continued on, but more slowly and carefully than before. Finding a narrow point in the trail, one he could defend without fear of being surrounded and where opponents would have to attack one at a time, he settled down to wait.

A day passed without event. Then, on the afternoon of the second day, Jerome was startled into full alertness when he simultaneously heard a group of Ronin approaching and felt the tingle of their accompanying Mushin.

As the Ronin came into view around a bend in the path, the fact of what he was about to attempt came home to him with full force. It wasn't simply a question of a physical battle with human opponents. He would also be fighting Mushin! If he allowed his mind control to slip for even a moment, if fear appeared on his mental horizon for the barest instant, he was doomed; the Mushin would swoop down on him and blast his mind into blazing Madness.

For a moment, he faltered, taking a step backward in dismay. Then he stopped. Looking to the right of him, he visualized Chaka standing there, calmly awaiting the attack, a fierce grin on her lips. He looked then to the left. The Old Master was there, an amused smile dancing from his eyes to his mouth and back again. Facing forward, raising his weapon toward the foe, he couldn't help letting a happy thought transform his own features. He laughed aloud. What beautiful clouds!

The Ronin stopped dead in their tracks as they caught sight of Jerome standing there, alone, directly in their path. There were three of them, in single file on the narrow way. Dumbfounded by the vision of a man, standing smiling waiting their coming with a mere stick in his hands, they simply stared for several moments in a frozen tableau.

Then the leading one snarled into action, ripping his sword from its sheath, leaping forward with a throaty howl.

The howl ended in a bloody gurgle as Jerome simply thrust forward with the blade of his weapon and cut the murderer's throat. The Ronin collapsed in a heap. The other two, their swords out and raised for the attack, came to an abrupt halt, the rear one crashing into the forward one. Quickly Jerome stepped forward, taking advantage of their confusion and lack of balance. He thrust at the leader, missing his heart by a fraction as the swordsman parried upward weakly with his blade. Jerome's blade flicked in and out of the man's shoulder, leaving a spreading stain behind.

But the Ronin was not down or out. The wound was in his left shoulder, so his sword arm was still usable. Recovering his balance, the swordsman threw himself forward, knocking Jerome's weapon upward with a blow from his sword. Blade on high he rushed in to deliver a slash at Jerome's head. But as the bladed end of Jerome's staff flew upward, the plain end simply circled around, the young man's hands acting as the pivot point, the power of his enemy's blow providing the momentum. The upward moving end dealt the descending blade a glancing blow, knocking it the crucial few inches to the right, causing the steel to bite thin air. The end of the staff, having blocked the sword and risen to the Ronin's eye level, suddenly struck out like a snake at the advancing man, smashing him squarely between the eyes.

Two killers lay dead.

The final Ronin had learned respect for the young man's weapon. Unorthodox it might be, but it was nonetheless for that deadly. He carefully backed toward a clear space to give himself more room to maneuver.

Mushin buzzed everywhere. Having feasted on the dying Ronin, they were in a feeding-frenzy. But search as they might, they could find no trace of Jerome's mind to attack. The young man's mental state was that which the Master had trained into him: a deep stillness coupled with an extended awareness. Jerome's sense of Self, securely centered in calmness, was at the same time fully merged with his environment, giving no hint of its presence to the mind leeches. Fear, terror, all emotions had evaporated into a cloud of quietude so profound that his mind was as invisible to the Mushin as they were to him. Frustrated, angry, even worried, they circled about in confusion.

The Ronin stepped in, delivering a 45-degree slash toward the right side of Jerome's neck. Stepping in and to his left at a similar angle, Jerome swept the bladed end of his weapon back and down, following the arc of the sword, gently moving it slightly to the right of its original trajectory. The force the sword exerted against the end of the staff brought it around even more swiftly and forcefully, the butt end rushing up and striking the Ronin on his right temple. The killer fell heavily, his head shattered by the blow.

For several silent moments, Jerome simply stood and looked at his fallen foe. Gradually, his mind returned to an ordinary state of consciousness. The Mushin sensed the return and pounced. One attempt, however, was enough to convince them there was nothing here to destroy. All was quietness. No sense of pride or fear or triumph came from the victor. Only a sense of relaxed calm existed. In frustration, the Mushin fled back up into the mountains, back to the Ronin refuge high up in the pass. Jerome sensed their departure and smiled.

Moving from one Ronin to the next, he collected all three swords. One by one he tried them, swinging them through the forms and techniques Father Ribaud had taught him in the Brotherhood. They all seemed about the same, but one had a slightly better feel, a finer sense of balance than the other two.

Deciding, he held it up over his head, watching the sun glint along the blade. He turned, keeping it aloft, as if showing it to the four horizons, hidden though they were behind the nearby walls of the mountains. His head tilted back he looked into the sky, watching the blade move against the clouds.

"I have it, Chaka," he said out loud. "I have it. And I'll use it. For you."

Chapter XIII

JEROME KNELT OVER the tracks. The four Ronin had stood here for several moments, probably deciding their next move. They must have realized they were being followed and might even have guessed who was on their trail. In any case, caution had prevailed and the quartet of killers had split up and gone their separate ways to elude pursuit. Perhaps they would meet again at some rendezvous, but it would be a long way off and Jerome had no idea in which direction it might lie.

He sat back on his haunches, automatically rearranging his sword for instant use. His hand moved further up the staff he carried to balance his shift in weight. His sun-darkened face was impassive.

The Ronin become more cautious, he mused. More and more careful. Now they creep about like tiny lizards raiding a 'steader's garden rather than rampaging like Ken-wolves ravishing a flock. He snorted, a grim smile flickering over his face. They have reason to tread lightly, he thought, reason to carry fear with them as they walk the secret forest ways. His free hand wandered over and gently touched the hilt of his sword.

Even if I haven't done anything else in the last four years, he told himself, I have taught the Ronin fear. He sighed softly as he stood. No sense in tracking this band any further. A lone Ronin wasn't that much of a threat to a family of 'steaders. Especially not now that so many were armed with the bladed staffs.

The idea had been Obie's actually. After Jerome had won his sword, he had given the weapon he had invented to the boy. Not quite knowing what to do with the two other swords he had taken from his dead opponents, he had left them in a corner of the cabin.

From time to time, the young man had drilled Obie in the use of the bladed staff, until the youth had become relatively proficient in its use. Then the boy had asked Jerome for the use of one of the swords and he had assented. Obie carefully constructed a new, improved version of the bladed staff with a longer blade and a metal knob at the opposite end to give it better balance. There was no question that Obie's weapon was superior to the original.

When Jerome killed three more Ronin and

brought home their swords, Obie set to work constructing more of the bladed weapons. Jerome was puzzled as to why the boy felt he needed four of them, but since he had no better use for the swords, he said nothing. Then Obie made his proposal, having plainly spent a lot of time thinking it out from every angle. It was simple, really. Arm the 'steaders with the bladed staffs. A few at a time. Teach them a basic manual of arms for the weapon and the rudimentary form of mind control necessary. Obie seemed sure most of the adults could learn both relatively easily. Eventually, every member of the family old enough to develop the necessary self-control could be taught. A family of four or more, the wife and children armed with lighter and shorter versions of the weapon, would be a bristling threat even to several Ronin. All that was required was for the family to keep their backs covered and their blades on guard.

A Ronin, even with a sword, was at a decided disadvantage even though the 'steaders were slower and less skilled. (Not that Ronin were exactly Masters of the Sword, Jerome reminded himself. They were dangerous not because of skill, but because of their utter disregard for life. They usually attacked all out, and under those circumstances, even a fool with a sharp sword is dangerous. Especially when his opponent is an unarmed, terrified 'steader.) A man with a sword had twice the distance to cover to deliver a blow as a 'steader with a bladed staff did. If he wasn't careful, a Ronin could end up impaling himself on his opponent's blade without ever even coming within striking distance. Generally, as long as the 'steaders remained cool, quietly repeating the Litany of Calmness to ward off the Mushin, the confrontation was a standoff.

Jerome smiled grimly again. Yes, the Ronin had reason to be afraid. For as well as training the 'steaders in the use of the bladed staff, he had hunted Ronin. And once the people in the valley had realized what Jerome was doing, they had tried to help in every way possible. Older children took to patrolling the woods when they weren't working with their families. As soon as Ronin or their trace were sighted, a relay of runners would carry the news to Jerome far more swiftly than the killers themselves could travel.

Within hours of an alarm anywhere in the valley, the young swordsman was on his way, tracking the marauders down. If the band was small enough, say only three or four, he would pick a good spot and ambush them. If there were more, he would expose himself and lead them on a chase, picking off one or two from hiding, until the total was low enough that he could make a stand against them. In this manner, he had killed over thirty Ronin within the last four years. New ones kept appearing, but ever fewer—and they were far more cautious.

Relieved from the constant threat of wandering bands of Mushin-driven killers, feeling safer with the bladed staffs in their hands, the 'steaders in the area had prospered. Jerome was revered and welcomed by everyone, and anything he and the children could not produce on their own farmstead, was willingly supplied by the grateful valley dwellers.

Chaka would be pleased, he thought. And although he himself was pleased, he wasn't satisfied. For even though he had brought peace to the valley, he had found no peace for himself. I'm doing what you asked, Chaka, he said silently. I'm moving with the flow. But for the life of me, I can't see that I'm getting anywhere. The answer to Nakamura's Koan doesn't seem four years closer. The Way to freedom is as hidden as ever.

That wasn't completely true, he admitted. What he had been doing had certainly freed the 'steaders to a great degree. But it was only a temporary thing, a stop-gap measure as transient as his own life. When I am gone, he lamented, even if they keep the tradition of the bladed staffs alive, the Ronin will increase again. No, the current situation was better, but it wasn't what the Koan promised. It wasn't true freedom from the Mushin and the Madness.

Looking back down the forest track he had been following in his pursuit of the Ronin, Jerome sighed again. Then he looked up through a break in the trees and saw the shining mountains that rimmed the valley. I wonder if the Old Master is still up there tending his garden, he thought.

He smiled, remembering the old man. How he would laugh to see Jerome teaching a 'steader how to handle a bladed staff without dropping it or cutting up his own family! Yet he knew the Master would approve. His own methods for teaching the sword would hardly work with the valley people! No, the weapon and the method were suitable for men without much time or training. And Jerome knew the old man would agree that any weapon was better than none at all. It's not the Way, he would say, Jerome mused, but all in all, it's as much the Way as anything else. He chuckled as he recalled the Master's brusque, enigmatic way of speaking. It's strange, he thought, how the things he said to me, things I didn't understand at all at the time, will come back to me, filled with new meaning. He shook his head in wonder. Maybe some day I'll actually understand it all. And all the things Chaka said. He snorted in self-derision. But that day seems a long way off!

Breaking his reverie, he began to trot back down the trail, heading for the River and the path that lead back toward his own 'stead.

As he came around a bend in the track, he heard a strange noise in the distance. Stopping, he listened carefully. It sounded like someone yelling. No, not yelling. Singing! Well, perhaps 'trying to sing' was a better description.

Curious, Jerome stepped off the track and hid among the bushes at the side of the faint road. Best always to be cautious. As he knelt in waiting, the song grew louder and other sounds were added to it in counterpoint. There was a squeaking, grating noise, and a huffing, lowing one. A rhythmic thumping kept up a constant background.

The sight that finally met his eyes as the source of the disturbance rounded the bend and came down the track toward his hiding place surprised him. One of the short, stubby Ken-cows led the way. It was decorated with tassles and colored ribbons. Behind it rumbled the most incredible cart Jerome had ever seen. Like the beast that drew it, it was covered with tassles and ribbons. In addition, it was piled high with a shapeless load covered by a multi-hued canvas-like sheet.

But the most astounding member of the group strode along next to the wagon, a long prod in his hand, his voice raised high in something resembling a mixture of song and bellowing. Jerome did not catch all of the words, but a good number of them were identical to those uttered in sniggering secrecy by the older boys behind the Refectory of the Brotherhood.

The singer was incredible. His robe was of the same cut as those worn by the Fathers and Brothers and by most of the 'steaders. Simple, falling straight from the shoulders to below the knees, it was hooded to cover the head in case of rain, and tied about the middle with a simple cord. But there the resemblance ended. This robe was a wild swirl of color, covered with dangling tassles and decked with bright ribbons, much the way the Ken-cow and cart were decorated.

Yet the most impressive thing about the man walking with the cart was his size. He was easily the largest human Jerome had ever seen. Not in height, no, for the stranger didn't reach Jerome's six feet by a good four inches. But in girth! The arms sticking out of the rolled-up sleeves of the robe were as big around as Jerome's thighs. The waist was unmeasurable. And the legs that showed beneath the bottom of the robe were mobile tree trunks.

Jerome stared in silent awe as the cart approached. When the singer was directly in front of him on the track, the man suddenly reached out, whacked the Ken-cow on the head with his prod and bellowed "Whoa, there, dammit! C'mon Pickle Puss, whoa!" Then he turned and stared directly into the eyes of the hidden Jerome.

"Well, well, damn my old eyes if I don't discover a skulker, a lurker in the Wood, mayhap even a Ronin? Nah, too calm for that! Who be you, lurker?" asked the singer in a rumbling voice.

Totally taken aback at being discovered, Jerome stood slowly and stepped out onto the track near the man. "Ho, a likely lookin' one! With a sword no less! Are he dangerous? No, not to the likes of me he aren't. I'm just a poor travelin' peddler, I am. Call me Sam, sir. Sam's as good as any name. How shall I call you?"

In some confusion, Jerome muttered, "I'm, uh, Jerome."

"And why be here in the Wood? Shouldn't you be home on the 'stead working? What do you think, Pickle Puss," he roared, addressing the Ken-cow, "shouldn't he be on his 'stead working? Tis dangerous wandering about in the Wood. Ronin, you know. Though come to think on it now, I've seen nary a one nor much sign of 'em for a time now."

Drawing himself up, Jerome replied, "I was tracking a party of Ronin. That's why I'm here in the Wood."

"Trackin' was he? My! Trackin' Ronin? Must be good with that sticker, eh?"

Jerome shrugged.

The peddler laughed hugely. "Ha, ha, ha, modest now! Oh, I love a modest man. So few of 'em, you know. Well, my good man, if you've nothin' more to do than wander about the Wood stalking Ronin, I could use a bit o' aid in the way of guiding and protection. This be my first trip into this area. Only just heard the rumors that it's safe here for the likes of a poor old peddler. Seems to be so, for I've seen nary a trace of Ronin now that I think on it.''

''Guiding? Protection? Guiding to where?''

''Well, man, don't be so slow. Quick now, lively up your mind!'' Old Sam waved a huge hand at his cart. ''There be all the fruits and benefits of civilization, such as they are on Kensho. Pots and pans, combs, mirrors, soap, seasonings, knives, hoes, shovels, pretties for the ladies, name it good sir, name it, and Old Sam will produce it forthwith beneath your very nose. But I need guiding to the 'steads in the area. Saves time to know where you're goin' before you go there. That's why guidin'. As for guardin', why, I worry a heap about the Ronin, poor old man like me, defenseless and all.''

Smiling at the genial volubility of the peddler, Jerome nodded. ''Why not? I can lead you to every farmstead around here. I know them all. But what do you expect to trade for? I mean, what do the 'steaders hereabouts have that you want for your wares?''

As they started walking along the track, Old Sam waved his ponderous arms and explained, ''No profit in it at all, my friend. 'Tis merely in the service of Mankind. I wander the face of this planet and bring the wonders of civilization to all and each. Course, I might accept a bit o' cloth of good weave now and then. Or some food products. Seems to me this area be a good one for Ko pods. And maybe I'll take me one or two of them Ronin-sticker things I've heard tell of. We don't have so many Ronin out on the Plain where I hail from, but might find a use for 'em anyway. And Boolay weed, natural, I'll take Boolay weed. Or Quizal what makes the aches in these old bones go way. Good market for Quizal on the Plain. Not much grows there any more. Oh, I'll take most anything in trade."

"Where do you get your wares from? I mean, you don't make the hoes and things yourself, do you? Don't they come from some Brotherhood?" queried Jerome.

"Course they do. Brotherhoods make 'em and give 'em away in their own neighborhood. But how's folks far away to benfit from a system like that? How's a 'steader way over by the Bay, going to get a hoe from the Brotherhood over to Razor-back Ridge, for that's where the best hoes be made? No ways, that's how, unless old Sam brings it to him. Aye, we peddlers are useful fellows and the Brotherhoods and 'steaders know it. We're the blood, so to speak, of Mankind here on Kensho, carrying things all over the body. And now as things seem to be gettin gettin' quieter and safer all the time, we can do our job. Oh, it was some sore trade bein' a peddler in the old days, friend. Dangerous it were! Many a good man cut down by Ronin."

"It's safer now in the Plain and Great Valley?" wondered Jerome.

"Surely. These last few years specially so. The numbers of Ronin be droppin'. Fewer lads turn Ronin now and almost none o' the lasses. Though I don't know why. And those that is Ronin seem not as wild as in the old days. More cold and cunning like. Not so crazy.

"And what with the Free Brotherhoods spreading now these last few seasons, there don't seem to be as many Mushin about neither. Makes peddlin' a sight easier."

"Free Brotherhoods?" asked Jerome. "What's a 'Free Brotherhood'?"

"Why one as has no Grandfather!" Old Sam stopped in surprise. "Surely you've heard of the Freeing? No? Ah, this is a virgin territory for a peddler, then! There's getting to be a sight too many of us back home."

"Freeing? What Freeing?" questioned Jerome. "I don't understand."

The peddler began walking along again. "Well, sir, it's like this. 'Bout eight or nine years ago a Brotherhood over in the Great Valley lost their Grandfather. The old Cockroach got himself killed by one of the Brothers no less! Well, it was a rough set-to as a result. Seems like no one was prepared for it. Lots of folks died, but in the end things settled down. Oh, hell, I can't give you all the details. I only know that with the Freeing there are fewer Mushin. Seems somehow the Grandfathers and the Mushin were connected. Or something like that. I forget. Anyway, that Freeing set off another. And another. Soon there must have been five or six Free Brotherhoods without no Grandfather. Ain't growing quite so fast now. Losses in a

Freeing are pretty high and . . . what's the matter, friend?''

Jerome had turned a deathly white beneath his deep tan. His mind raced back to that day so long ago when he had sat in the Grandfather's cell. Shivering at the memory, he recalled how the creature had tried to invade his mind. He remembered his soundless struggle to maintain his control, the sudden realization that somehow the Grandfathers, the benefactors of Mankind, were linked to the Mushin, Man's greatest enemy.

He shook himself out of the past, but still in a corner of his mind he watched the young Brother flee the Brotherhood in the night and begin his trek up the side of the Mountain to the hut of the Master.

''What be wrong, sir? You look as if you'd seen Mushin! Be you sick? I've medicine of sorts in the cart.''

Jerome shook his head. ''No, no, I'm all right now. I . . . I just remembered something that happened many years ago. I'm all right now.''

''Whew, what a fright you give me, friend!''

For a moment the two walked on in a strained silence. Old Sam looked at Jerome from the corner of his eye. Several times he made as if to speak, but decided not to and merely mumbled to himself. Finally he stopped and turned.

''You said your name was Jerome?'' His companion nodded. ''Hmmmmmm. You know Waters Meeting? Ah, I see you do! Does the name Ribaud mean anything to you?''

Jerome literally went rigid. ''Ribaud?'' he asked in a hiss. ''You know Ribaud?'' Unthinking, his hand touched the hilt of his sword.

Instantly the manner of Old Sam changed. The prod became an obvious weapon in his hands, his ponderous body cat-like in its tense readiness. His face hardened and his voice softened. "Carefully now, Jerome. Calm. I'm a friend."

"Ribaud. Tell me about Ribaud."

"Ah. You are not just Jerome. You are *the* Jerome. We wondered if it was you when we heard rumors of changes out here on the frontier, of Ronin being wiped out, of 'steaders being armed and trained, of the Mushin fear being pushed back and back. Ribaud thought you might be responsible."

Jerome's jaw dropped. "What? Responsible? I . . . but . . ." he stuttered in confusion.

The old man ignored him. "Ribaud and the rest of the Council of the Free Brotherhoods asked us to keep an eye peeled for you in our journeys. We were all given the same message to deliver should we find you. 'Go to the Free Brotherhood at Waters Meeting. Ribaud needs you.' I know nothing more. The rest is dark secret that Ribaud will explain."

Sam sighed hugely, his serious demeanor falling away like a dropped shawl. "Ah, 'tis sad to be losin' my guide and guard. But somehow this poor defenseless old man will have to make do." He jiggled he beribboned sleeve at Jerome. "Oh, off with you! I'll make me own way in this howling wilderness!"

Without waiting for another word, he turned, prodded the Ken-cow into motion and rumbled off down the track.

For several moments Jerome stood silently, staring after the retreating figure of the old peddler. His stillness masked the furious action of his mind. Ribaud! Alive! And asking to see him! It could be a trick, of course, a ruse to lure him back and take revenge for the death of the Grandfather.

But Sam had spoken as if the death of the Grandfather was a good thing, an act the Fathers were thankful for. And he had mentioned that others had been killed, that other Brotherhoods had gotten rid of their alien rulers! The Freeing, he had called it. And Sam's whole demeanor was too absurd to be anything but real.

I can't leave, though, he thought. The valley needs me. I'm the only thing that stands between them and the Ronin. And there's Obie and Misako and Tommy, too. They need me.

Clearly, inside his mind, he heard Chaka's mocking laughter. Oh, how important, how serious we are, her voice called out sarcastically. The whole world will cease, the sun will fail to rise, if we do not get up and chirp in the morning like a good little tree lizard.

Jerome chuckled, warmed by the memory of the girl's good-natured needling. Flow, she had told him again and again. Flow. And indeed it seemed as if the current was running in the direction of the Brotherhood at Waters Meeting. The 'steaders could survive quite well without him for a while. And the children would be watched over carefully during his absence. Obie had been talking about organizing a flying squad of bladed-staff wielders to supplement Jerome's own efforts. This would be a good time to attempt the venture.

No, the valley didn't depend solely on him any longer. And Ribaud's call was intriguing to say the least. It must be important if they were making such a widespread effort to find him again.

I'll go, he decided. It feels like the right thing to do. Turning, he headed through to the woods toward his 'stead by the most direct path. No time like the present to get started, he thought. I'll pick up a few things at the cabin and be off by midafternoon.

CHAPTER XIV

THE LIGHT OF noon painted the world in harsh tones of blank wall and black shadow. Every charred timber held a sense of stark and hard-edged reality that bruised the mind. There was no doubting what had happened. In dismay, Jerome stared about at the ruins of the Brotherhood.

Slowly he turned back to the figure that stood patiently waiting, every detail on his worn robe picked out with uncompromising clarity by the harsh sun. "It's hard to accept, Father," he mumbled.

"Yes. But there's no alternative. It happened. Many died. We've left these ruins as they are to remind us how irrevocable the past is. It can't be changed." Ribuad smiled sadly. "Nor would I change it if I could. Much good has come of evil in a way none of us ever expected."

Ribaud sat on the ruined wall of the Meditation Hall and motioned to Jerome to sit next to him. "There's pain in remembering," he continued, "but it's honest pain and if felt and let go again, it causes no lasting harm.

"It was just too sudden, Jerome. We didn't expect it. When the morning came and you were nowhere to be found, I sent a Novice to search you out. Everyone was nervous. The number of Mushin hovering about was incredible.

"The lad finally decided you must still be with the Grandfather. He crept up to the door and peeked through a crack, fearful of disturbing the Grandfather, but desirous of fulfilling his errand. What he saw was too much for a mind with as little training as his. A headless Grandfather!" Ribaud sighed. "Poor lad. He was swamped by the Mushin, instantly driven into raving lunacy. He came screaming into the Meditation Hall and fell, clawing and biting, on several Sons who were engaged in their Morning Sitting.

"Well, it was like a chain reaction. One set the other off. The Mushin rushed in from everywhere, driven to a frenzy by such a feast of madness. They actually attacked! They didn't just hang around waiting for an opening as they usually do. They tried to drive their way into our minds, tried to tear an opening in our defenses." Grimly Ribaud looked around at the devastation. "That must have been what it was like when they hit our ancestors at First Touch, when we came down from the Arks."

"How . . . how many died," faltered Jerome.

"Forty-eight," came the quiet reply. "Forty-eight out of seventy-four."

For a moment, they sat silent beneath the bright sun, each feeling the shape of his own sadness. To the old man, this was nothing new. He had been living with it for many years. Now it was a mere sadness remembered, a soft melancholy that bore only a dull ache rather than searing pain. And besides, seeing Jerome again, so much alive, so strong, so matured, was a joy that easily overcame dull aches. There is hope in such as these, he assured himself. There is hope.

Pulling himself from his reverie, he continued his tale. "No need for a blow by blow description. As soon as I realized what was happening, I rushed to the practice yard to get to the swords before the Mad Ones did. I was too late. Perhaps if I'd been five minutes earlier, the carnage would have been less. Who knows? Father Angelo and I gathered together the sane and semi-sane and fled into the fields. From there we watched the slaughter and burning. By late afternoon it was over. It took much longer to bury them than it had for them to kill each other.

"So now we're a Free Brotherhood. One of six, plus the three Free Sisterhoods. And thankful for it."

"I don't understand. A Free Brotherhood? And thankful for so many deaths?"

Ribaud grinned. It seemed strange, following such a tale of horror. "Tell me, Jerome, do you sense any Mushin about? No? Isn't it strange, considering that now more than thirty of us live here in the ruins of the Brotherhood? More than thirty souls and not one hopeful, hungry Mushin hovering around?

"We don't completely understand it. Perhaps it's the inevitable result of a baptism by fire like a Freeing. The fact of it is, though, that those of us who survived the experience aren't bothered by the Mushin any longer! We're free! It's not something we planned, not something we strove for. It just happened.

"Of course we were trained followers of the Way of Passivity. But the Way did us no good when the assault came. For the force with which the Mushin struck was beyond the strength of any little miserable walls of defense we might have built up by following the Way of Passivity.

"Wall, walls, walls! We all lived behind walls, Jerome! The Grandfathers taught us how and we built them in our fear! But walls are not enough, they're never strong enough. Never! We should have known that. Just looking around at the world would have shown us that. The mighty Ko tree is toppled by a mightier wind. But the reed bends and is saved. The little water lizard that lives in the mountain stream doesn't build a solid nest to resist the current. His home is open to the flow and is never washed away by even the strongest flood.

"Forty-eight of us were doomed because the violence that our walls kept within was as great as the hunger for it which lurked without. But the rest of us, through no intention, and thanks to no training, had built our walls around calmness. When the Mushin penetrated the defenses, they found nothing there to feed on. We survived because of what we were, at our very cores, not because of what we had made ourselves.

"I wish there could have been some easier, less lethal way for us to find what we really are." He sighed, "but with the Mushin and the Grandfathers and the teaching of the Way . . ." his voice trailed off into a thoughtful silence.

"You question the Way of Passivity, Father?"

Ribaud nodded. "Yes, yes, I have no choice. Oh, I know you told me so, many years ago. I remember how you questioned it all, the Grandfathers, the Way, the whole thing, But I didn't see it then. There was no focus for my own doubts. Now it all seems so clear."

Another silence descended upon the two men seated on the ruined wall. Ribaud gazed quietly inward, his eyes abstract, dreamy and faraway. Jerome's brow was wrinkled, his eyes hooded in thought, his hands absently playing with his Smoothstone as they often did when he was concentrating.

Finally, the younger man began to speak, softly at first, but his voice gaining in strength and conviction as he continued. "Father, there's another possible explanation for why the Mushin no longer bother you here at the Free Brotherhood. Did you have a chance to examine the corpse of the Grandfather before the Brotherhood burned? No? Well, I did. It was hollow. The whole thing, head and all, was an empty shell!

"I mentioned this once to a friend of mine, a girl. I also told her that just before I struck the Grandfather, I perceived some sort of link between the Grandfather and the Mushin. Yes! A link! Father, the Grandfather tried to take over my mind. He invaded it the way the Mushin do. Softer, more subtle, but similar.

"Oh, yes, there's one more piece of information you need to see my point. Out on the 'steads, there are hardly any Mushin. The mind leeches tend to cluster around the Brotherhoods and Sisterhoods.

"Knowing all this, Chaka, the girl, had an idea. What you just told me confirms it. She thought that perhaps the Grandfathers were really just creatures of the Mushin the way the Ronin are. It all fits. The Mushin attacked us at First Touch and very nearly wiped us out. Then they must have realized that if they weren't careful, they would completely annihilate us, destroying an invaluable food source.

"So the Mushin hit on a strategem. The Grandfathers. And the Way of Passivity. They took our best, the dangerous ones with enough intelligence to perhaps figure out their plan, and brought them together in the Brotherhoods and Sisterhoods, drilling them in the disciplines of the Way. Not only did this misdirect their energy from seeking a way of escape, the Way of Nakamura's Koan, but it also provided the Mushin with a constant, controlled food source. As you said, most of the walls we built simply contained violence, hatred, greed, desire, frustration . . . all the emotions the Way was supposed to get rid of, but which it only repressed instead. And all those repressed emotions made the Brotherhoods and Sisterhoods ever-fruitful sources of food for the Mushin.

"As I see it, Father, the Mushin use the Grandfathers to control the Brotherhoods, to make sure we don't stray from the Way of Passivity, to assure that new ideas are repressed and the system is maintained. The Grandfathers aren't really alive at all. They're only interfaces between the Mushin and humanity. Men open their minds willingly in the presence of a Grandfather. They're the mind leeches' way of communicatiing with us, giving us instructions, keeping us in line.

"For some seven generations, since the Madness struck at First Touch, the Grandfathers have been the link that perpetuates a mutual accommodation between our two species. We're allowed to continue to exist at the price of serving as food for the Mushin."

Ribaud looked pale and slightly ill. "Food. Herded like Ken-cows by hollow interfaces to feed invisible mind leeches." His voice died out in a mumble. For several moments he sat and stared at the ground.

Finally he looked up, the hard light glinting in his eyes. "That would explain why they haven't returned—but it still seems true that only those who were calm at their Center survived the initial Freeing. It's possible to be free of the Mushin if one is free of the Grandfathers. And if one is calm enough to survive the Freeing.

"But what you've revealed to me does fit. We've created a crisis we didn't even know about. Your whole theory requires one more idea to make it completely plausible: that the Mushin are intelligent! Not just savage, senseless mind destroyers, but clever creatures capable of realizing a problem existed and thinking out a solution! And what a solution! Gods, Jerome, it's a master stroke! What the Grandfathers said about taking the Way out of Nakamura's mind as he lay dying must have been true! Where else would they have been able to find a scheme so perfectly tailored to human modes of thought? Even if all the Pilgrims weren't followers of the Universal Way of Zen, they knew about it and were familiar with its teachings. So the Mushin adapted it to suit their needs while making it seem to fit ours!''

Ribaud shook his head in wonder. ''But what a dilemma this creates! It makes everything much more urgent. Perhaps only luck has saved us this far. Why, they could be preparing a counterattack at this very moment!''

Jerome looked puzzled. ''Counterattack? By whom? Against what?''

The old man hunched his shoulders and looked about fearfully. ''The Mushin. Look, Jerome, we've been freeing Brotherhoods by destroying the Grandfathers. Six in all. And three Sisterhoods. But we've stopped because the losses are so terrible, so great. Each time almost two-thirds die, horribly. We're exhausted. The Free Brotherhoods still haven't regained their previous production levels, and the 'steaders are suffering as a result.

''But at least so far, the Mushin haven't reacted. They've never made any attempt to reassert their control over a Free Brotherhood. We never had any reason to suppose they would. After all, if they were just wild, mindless creatures . . .'' His voice trailed off for a moment.

"This revelation of yours, though, changes all that. If the Mushin are intelligent, if the Grandfathers are their control interfaces with our race, why, they're bound to react sooner or later.'' Ribaud shuddered. "I can't imagine what they'll do, but the very thought . . . I don't know if we'd be able to fend them off, we're so weak and so few. I just don't know.''

Sighing deeply, the old man looked back at Jerome. "I sent for you because I had a mission for you. One I believe only you can accomplish. My original purpose was, I admit, more a question of curiosity than anything else. Now it may be a matter of survival! It means a long journey, one that's bound to be dangerous and that may well end in failure. But suddenly it's become very urgent—it just may give us the key we need to save ourselves. It may lead to the Way mentioned in Nakamura's Koan.''

His face alert with interest, Jerome stood and smiled. "When do I leave?'' he asked.

Ribaud smiled back, relief plain in his look. "First I have to call several people together so we can tell you about it. That'll take some time. We have to send for Mother Cynthia. But come. You can to eat while we wait.'' He rose from his sitting place, gesturing Jerome to follow. Slowly the two of them threaded their way through the ruins to the Refectory which still stood and was now the center of the Free Brotherhood. In a few moments they disappeared into cool depths, leaving the charred timbers and harsh sun to stare at each other.

It was three hours before the group that Ribaud had called to the meeting had all arrived. Having the furthest to travel, Mother Cynthia was the last. A swift runner had made it to the Sisterhood in less than an hour, but Cynthia was old and slow. Finally she huffed into the Refectory and plumped down with an oath at the long table where the rest were already seated.

Ribaud began. ''This group is the Council of the Free Brother- and Sisterhoods. A few members are missing since they're just too far to call on such short notice. But we've a quorum, so, to business.

''Fathers, and Mother Cynthia, I have some very grim news. On the basis of information Jerome has brought, I've reason to believe that the Mushin are intelligent. You can surmise the significance of that yourselves, I imagine.''

For a moment, stunned silence filled the room. Then it was ripped by an excited buzzing of voices. ''The devil you say!'' cried grizzled Father Nostra, the Smith of the Brotherhood. ''Intelligent? Nah! How came you to that idea?''

Slowly and carefully, Jerome repeated the reasoning he had earlier expounded to Ribaud. When he had finished another silence settled over the group, but this time it was a thoughtful one.

''If what you say is true, lad,'' spoke up Father Wilson, ''and for all of me I can't find an error in your reasoning, then we've a real mess on our hands.''

"Aye," called out another. "Only six Brother-hoods and three Sisterhoods are free. We've lost over 300 in those Freeings and virtually crippled our output of tools and food. In all, we number about 150 Free Brothers and Sisters. That's not many. At least not enough to withstand a con-certed attack by an intelligent enemy."

"That's the nub of it," nodded Ribaud. "Nine Freeings are sure to have alerted the Mushin that something is up. If they're intelligent, they're bound to respond."

"Perhaps the best defense is an attack. Perhaps we should begin a new wave of Freeings im-mediately," suggested Father Gonzales. "We could create so much confusion that they might hesitate to counterattack. We might gain breathing space that way."

Mother Cynthia snorted. "Ha. We'd never sur-vive a new wave of Freeings. It'd let chaos loose on the land. Better we all perish than that we destroy the whole of Mankind. No, we got our-selves into this mess. We have to get ourselves out, not just make the mess worse."

Ribaud looked appraisingly at the assembled Fathers. Then he turned to Jerome. "What do you think, my Son?"

His brow furrowed in thought, Jerome looked down at the tabletop. "Well," he began hesi-tantly, "first of all, you're assuming the Mushin are intelligent. That's not necessarily the case. I remember Father Ross, the Teaching Master here at Waters Meeting, telling us about an Earth crea-ture called an 'ant'. These little animals herded another little creature called an 'aphid'. They used them to gather the juice of certain plants. No one ever claimed the ants were intelligent just because they herded other animals.

"But here, I admit, the *method* is what seems to indicate intelligence. The Mushin use the Grandfathers to communicate with us, to impress the Way of Passivity on us in order to keep us in line. This seems to imply conscious direction. It also seems difficult to conceive of how they could have created the Way unless they were intelligent, even if they did steal it from Nakamura's mind.

"Overall, I suppose, the wisest course of action would be to assume the enemy is intelligent. At least that way we won't be guilty of underestimating him.

"The next thing is to try and figure out what the Mushin would do to counteract the Freeings. Again, assuming that they even care."

"Ronin," muttered Father Connark. Everyone at the table looked at him. "Ronin. We've long known the Mushin control the Ronin in some way. Surely the Ronin seek out the Mushin. If the Mushin do control them, what's to prevent them from assembling a mob of Ronin and attacking the Free Brotherhoods? We couldn't hold them off, we're too weak right now."

"Could be that's why we've had so few Ronin around of late," someone mused. "Could be the Mushin are massing them for an attack."

"Why bother with Ronin? What if Mushin alone attack? By the millions—submerge us, bury us, tear our minds to shreds. If there were enough of 'em and they kept at it for long enough, I doubt many of us'd survive. Lord, I know I barely made it through the Freeing. What I'm talking about would be a million times as bad.'' Father Nostra glared about at the others. ''Any one o' you thinks he could withstand that kind of onslaught?''

Everyone muttered vaguely and looked down at the tabletop, afraid to meet the doubt in his neighbor's eyes.

Ribaud was the first to break the new silence. ''In either case, we're ill-prepared to meet the threat. And even supposing the threat is unreal, what have we really accomplished? What have the Freeings achieved? Does anyone here really think they're the way to save our race from the Mushin?'' Shaking heads and murmured negatives ran around the table.

Wilson sighed. ''It seems we're at an impasse. If the Mushin are intelligent, we're doomed. If they aren't we're nearly as bad off. Oh, I agree, the Freeings have done a world of good for those of us who've survived. But we can't doom two-thirds of the human population on Kensho! Thank God there are no Mushin about right now, for I'm feeling depressed enough to provide an easy opening.''

''Fathers,'' Ribaud said quietly, ''are you willing to try the scheme I've several times proposed?''

''Ah, Ribaud, it's folly!'' exclaimed Father Nostra. ''Who'd we send for the task? Even if a task there truly be? I say the Knowledge is legend, nothing more.''

Connark looked quickly from Jerome to Ribaud. "Jerome? You'd send Jerome?"

Ribaud nodded firmly. "I'd send Jerome. That's why I sent out the call with the peddlers. I know something the rest of you don't."

The old man turned to Jerome. "Have you still got the medallion that was around your neck that morning I found you at Waters Meeting?" Nodding, Jerome reached inside his robe, pulled forth the medallion, lifted it off over his head, and handed it to Ribaud. The latter took it and held it up for all to see. "This, Fathers, if I'm not mistaken, is the identity tag of a crew member from one of the Arks. It says, 'P. Rausch, Chief Engineer.' That's followed by a long number of some sort. It's the only one of its kind I've ever seen or heard of. Jerome says it's been handed down in his family from father to son ever since the beginning of our stay on Kensho."

The medallion passed around the table. Nostra looked it over carefully, "Strange metal, this. Never seen the likes. Are you thinking, Ribaud, it'll give him access to the Arks?"

"I'm betting my life on it," Ribaud replied grimly.

"Aye, and his and everyone else's too," mumbled the Smith.

Connark handed the medallion back to Jerome. "But even if the badge gives him access, how's he to get there? You know what the Knowledge says: 'The Way is guarded by Mindless Ones, ten to the tenth in power. None may enter who Desire, to see the Master in his tower.'"

"I'm aware of that, too," Ribaud answered. "But of all of us, Jerome stands the best chance. The rest of us have been followers of the Way of Passivity, a Way chosen for us by our enemies. Only Jerome has walked a Way of his own choosing—the Way of the Sword. His is the only active Way. The warning is to those who have followed the passive Way. I hope, I pray, that an active Way will bring success where the passive has failed." He turned to Jerome. "What do you think?"

Jerome smiled. "About what? I'm lost. What's this 'Knowledge' you're all talking about?"

Father Wilson laughed. "Ha! See, we've taken you in as one of us. So much so that we forget you don't know everything we know! The Knowledge is an oral tradition, passed on, secretly, from one generation to another among those deemed suited. The Grandfathers knew nothing of it. Oh, it goes on and on, a lot of it garbled nonsense. But central to it is the idea that salvation for Mankind on Kensho somehow lies within the Arks. But it warns of the dangers of the guarding Mushin and says none can enter who lack the Key. We'll tell you the whole of it. Mother Cynthia knows the thing by heart."

"The long and short of it is, though," interrupted Ribaud, "that I think 'the place where he dwelt before he was born' mentioned in the Koan, refers to the Arks. That's where we all came from before we were born on this planet. And I think that's where Nakamura hid something we can fight the Mushin with. I believe that's what the Koan means, Jerome. And now it's more crucial than ever that we find out. What we want you to do is try and enter the Arks and seek out the weapon the Admiral may have hidden there to save mankind. It's . . . it's . . ." his voice faltered, "it's our only hope."

"You're sending him to his death," thundered Nostra.

Jerome sat, his head down. A strange warm feeling was growing in his lower abdomen. It wasn't fear, that much he knew. But he couldn't quite identify it. Go to the Arks. Go to seek the Way. He was qualified. He had studied the active Way, the Way of the Sword, with the Old Master on the Mountain. He had always been strangely immune to the Mushin, even on the night of his parents' massacre and the night when he had struck and killed the Grandfather. On the Mountain, he had been close to the Madness several times, thanks to the beatings the Master had given him. *But he had never fallen prey to the Mushin!* In combat with the Ronin during his wanderings, he had never been invaded by the mind leeches. He had always killed coolly, calmly.

Suddenly he recognized the growing warmth in his middle. It was joy! This was right, as right as water running downhill! This was the flow Chaka had spoken of so often. His Way led to the Arks! He knew it! It was not out of Desire he went, but out of the same kind of need that made him drink when he was thirsty, sleep when he was tired. Like the stream the Master had spoken of, Jerome must wend his way to the Sea.

He looked up at the solemn Fathers and laughed delightedly. Ribaud, ah, dear old Ribaud! The man who had first placed the sword in his hands looked so sad and so proud at the same time. He wanted to go along, but knew he could not. And crusty old Nostra! Worried and angry at Ribaud for sending him off on such a dangerous mission. And all the rest, concerned about someone they hardly knew but loved just because he was one of them.

His laughter bubbled down into a smile. "I'll leave in the morning. But tonight you must feed me well and tell me all about this Knowledge of yours!"

Another departure, he thought. But this time it would lead to the beginning!

CHAPTER XV

FIRST TOUCH. Jerome stood on a ridge top and looked down at the place where the Pilgrims had landed to construct Base Camp. The place where the Mushin had first struck the unprepared humans. Where the slavery of his race to the mind leeches had begun.

It wasn't very impressive.

In seven generations, most of the half-completed buildings had collapsed and become grass-covered mounds. Ironically the one-way transports, even though they had been partially dismantled by the Pilgrims, looked in far better shape than the powerful rocket shuttles that had been used to bring down heavy gear. Light-weight plastics and ceramics had stood up to the assaults of salt-laden sea air; the "sturdy" shuttles with their almost entirely metallic construction were in an advanced state of decomposition.

Far more awe-inspiring than remains of the meager works of Man was Jerome's first sight of the sea. Its calm blueness, dotted with the white ruffles of waves, swept on to the horizon. Here was a blue majesty to match the purple grandeur of the mountains in the interior.

Here was patience and power such as he had never felt before. For several moments, he stood gazing thoughtfully. Then, with a sigh, he returned his attention to the pathetic ruins of Base Camp. Immediately he noticed something strange: a band of bare soil, approximately a half-mile wide, completely surrounded the Camp and adjacent transports and shuttles. Outside the band the grass and shrubs of the Plain grew in their usual profusion. Inside the band, covering the mounded debris and growing beneath and around the ships, the plant life appeared equally lush. But the band itself, a huge ring that circled the area of Base Camp, totally devoid of life.

No, wait. There was something moving out there. Just coming around from the opposite side of the shuttles to the right of the Camp proper, trudging along the outer edge of the band, were three men.

Jerome dropped to the ground and crawled back to the opposite side of the rise. Hidden, he watched as the men continued their circuit, coming closer and closer to the ridge behind which he hid.

They carried swords! And by the tattered state

of their clothing, they looked like Ronin!

Ronin? Three Ronin calmly patrolling the perimeter of the ring of empty ground? For, that, without any doubt, was exactly what the trio was doing. But why? It made no sense. There wasn't a farmstead within a day's journey of this spot, so they weren't here to prey on 'steaders. What kept them endlessly circling?

At their closest approach, the three were no more than 200 yards from where Jerome lay hidden by obscuring growth. He hugged the ground, held his breath, and blanked his mind to give no hint of his presence to either the Ronin or their attendent Mushin. They passed and continued their circuit.

He waited patiently while the trio completed another turn around the ring to verify his suspicion. There seemed no doubt about it. The Ronin were guarding the approach to the ruins of Base Camp and the rusting hulks of the ships.

This was something Ribaud and the others had not prepared him for. The Knowledge, which Mother Cynthia had spent all evening chanting and commenting on, had intimated, poetically, that Mushin guarded the ships. Nothing had been said of human sentinels.

Jerome slid farther down his side of the slope. This bore thinking on. He wasn't too worried about his ability to handle the three Ronin. He had once killed a group of five. But was he up against anything as simple as three swordsmen? Or did the ring of bare earth mean he was up against something more?

What was the ring? A vague idea gnawed at the back of his mind, telling him he should recognize the patch of empty ground, should know its meaning. He felt keenly that the knowledge was important.

Suddenly it came to him: the ring resembled the Emptiness, the lifeless area around the Grandfather's cell in each of the Brotherhoods! The Emptiness was something the aliens insisted on, though they offered no explanation as to why it was necessary and no human had any idea why it was so important to them. As a Novice, Jerome himself had often patrolled the area with a poisonous solution, finding and eradicating every tiniest sign of life.

All right, he reasoned, the ring resembles the Emptiness and perhaps the resemblance goes beyond appearance. Perhaps they both have the same purpose. What could that purpose be? Whatever it was, the Grandfathers required it. Did the circling Ronin require it for similar reasons, he wondered?

Wait a minute—of course! The Grandfathers and the Ronin have one thing in common; they're both creatures of the Mushin. Which seemed to indicate that the real importance of the ring and the Emptiness was related to the Mushin rather than to either the Grandfathers or the Ronin.

But why would an empty, dead, lifeless area be necessary to the mind leeches? For several moments, he puzzled over the question. Then, finding no answer at hand, he decided to backtrack and see if he had overlooked some crucial bit of evidence.

The Grandfathers seemed like a logical place to begin, he thought. Perhaps there was some little fact about them that would supply the key. Going back in his mind to his long-ago interview with the alien, he remembered the phrase the creature has used to refer to itself: "vessel of totality." It hadn't meant anything to him at the time, but now it seemed significant.

The Grandfathers were merely interfaces between the Mushin and humanity. So it seemed that the word "vessel" was quite appropriate as a description of the Grandfathers' function. Did that mean, he wondered, that "totality" referred to the Mushin?

Totality? He knew there were individual Mushin, or at least that there was more than one. The invisible mind leeches could be found in many places at the same time. So why use the word "totality" to refer to themselves? Slowly an idea began to form in his mind. Could it be that although they were not a singular mentality, they might be a collective one? Or perhaps an aggregative one? Maybe an individual Mushin was too weak to accomplish much. Perhpas only when they had gathered together and become a "totality", were they intelligent and powerful enough to achieve anything. He remembered that the mind leeches always seemed to come in clumps or groups, swarming around the mind in huge numbers, battering away at its defenses.

If the Mushin were some kind of collective entity or mentality, that explained the function of the Grandfathers. The description of them as "vessels of totality" indicated that they were a focusing mechanism, through which a group or "totality" of Mushin could focus their combined power in a very precise way.

Still, he pondered, that didn't explain the purpose or meaning of the Emptiness or the ring.

Or did it? he suddenly realized. After all, the Mushin responded to emotive energy. Fed off it, to be exact. It seemed likely that before Mankind had come to Kensho, the mind leeches had lived on the indigenous flora and fauna. That, he calculated, meant they must be sensitive to the emotive emanations of local life-forms as well as to those of men. In the presence of strong emotions, he knew, the Mushin often went wild, bursting into a feeding-frenzy, losing all control. That was the extreme case, of course, but perhaps the emotive output of even minor life-forms disturbed the control of the Mushin, making it difficult for them to concentrate.

If that was the case, he continued to himself, then an area without life would be extremely useful to the Mushin. For example, the Emptiness surrounding the Grandfathers would be devoid of emotive interference from other life forms, allowing the mind leeches to concentrate their own forces with as few distractions as possible. Also it would minmize the danger of the death throes of some animal sparking off a feeding frenzy that would result in the Mushin destroying their stock of human cattle.

Assume that is the function of the Emptiness, he postulated; given the similarity between the area around First Touch and the Emptiness, it seemed to follow that the ring had the same purpose. That meant that the Mushin would be able to concentrate their forces within the barren space. Also, they would be able to direct those forces with far greater intelligence.

This must be the danger the poetry of the Knowledge had hinted at. Jerome remembered again the size of the empty ring the Ronin patrolled. Mentally he compared it to the size of the area around the Grandfather's cell. The result wasn't very reassuring. The ring was bigger, thousands of times bigger. If the area was directly proportional to the intensity of the Mushin concentration . . .

Oh well, he shrugged, trying to convince himself with his own casualness. I knew I'd have to come up against the Mushin sooner or later in order to reach my goal. There's nothing to do but do it.

The question of the ring and its meaning resolved, at least to his own satisfaction, he turned back to the problem of the Ronin. He didn't think he really wanted to tackle both the concentrated force of the Mushin and the swords of the killer trio at the same time; that meant he'd have to lure the Ronin out of the circle.

Given the nature of the beast, that didn't appear to pose an insurmountable difficulty. The sight of one man was generally enough to send three Ronin into a killing rage. To make sure of their response, Jerome decided on a ruse.

Carefully he climbed back up to the crest again and peered over. The guards were a quarter of the way around the circle, headed away from him.

Soon they would be lost to sight behind the debris of First Touch. Jerome readied himself. He untied his sword and scabbard and pulled them from the sash that circled his waist.

As the Ronin disappeared behind the Arks, he sprinted down the slope to a point near the circle where a small bush stood. Quickly he arranged his sword in the grass, covering it so it was invisible from a short distance. Then he lay down behind the bush.

His plan was simplicity itself. When the Ronin had come as close to where he lay as their circuit would bring them he would rise, weaponless. They would undoubtedly rush to the attack, out of the circle. At the last moment he would reach down into the grass and draw his sword. His skill, added to the element of surprise, should be sufficient.

As the trio approached Jerome unconsciously held his breath, willing himself to total invisibility behind his inadequate cover. He needed all the surprise he could achieve to push them into a hasty, ill-considered action. If they saw him too soon, they'd have time to think about the oddness of the situation before they reached him. Slowly, slowly, they advanced.

Now! In one swift motion he stood, empty-handed. He felt a thrill run up his spine as the three heads turned and three pairs of eyes gazed at him. The urge to grab up his sword was almost too strong to resist: unarmed in front of three Ronin!

But the thrill rapidly turned to dismay. The Ronin did not come howling to the kill. Slowly, their eyes riveted on him, they continued on their circuit to the point nearest him. At that point, one of the three halted, drew his sword, and turned to face him. The other two turned their heads and continued on their rounds.

Jerome could barely believe his eyes. This was not the way of Ronin. This was not the manner of the thrill-killers at all! His mind raced, confused, worried—and yet fascinated. This was something new and utterly unexpected.

He bent to pick up his sword, keeping his eyes on the Ronin the while. Carefully he placed the scabbard back into his sash and tied the cords. Then he walked slowly toward the Ronin who stood, sword on-guard in a very professional-looking manner, about ten feet inside the ring.

Quite evidently there was no way to attack the Ronin without moving inside the ring. As a test, he walked to a point some fifteen feet further along the ring. The guard silently followed, still within the ring. Jerome sighed. Well, then it had to be within the ring.

The other Ronin were just rounding the curve and disappearing again. Why hadn't they stayed? Obviously, the Mushin believed one guard was adequate. Against most men, he probably would be.

Jerome looked him over; the Ronin appeared likely to be a tough fighter, a worthy opponent. Too worthy?

Jerome drew his own sword and stepped up to the edge of the ring. "Come no further, man," the Ronin suddenly spoke. Jerome froze in his tracks, amazed. He'd never know a Ronin to warn a victim. They never spoke, just shrieked and struck. "Come not within the ring. It is forbidden for those of your race to come within the ring."

"My race? Mine? Are you not a man?" Jerome asked.

For a brief moment a look of confusion passed over the Ronin's visage. Then it settled back into its cold calmness. "No. I am a servant to Totality. Come not within. The ring is forbidden for those of your race.

"Servant of Totality, I have an appointment with Admiral Nakamura," Jerome said with mock gravity.

Again the Ronin looked momentarily confused. "Come not within the ring, man. It is . . ."

"I know, I know. 'Forbidden for those of my race.' But it's been too long a trip to turn back now. So if you'd just step aside . . ."

"Come not within the ring, man."

Jerome stepped within the ring.

CHAPTER XVI

IT WAS LIKE sticking his head into a hot oven. The burning pressure of untold numbers of Mushin hit his mind with a force he had never imagined. He reeled beneath the impact, fighting desperately for control. This was no gentle probing or careful prying at weak spots, but a smashing, battering assault intended to crush his mind out of existence. There was no interest in feeding. The purpose was plainly annihilation.

As Jerome staggered, the Ronin took a step toward him. He almost laughed. It looked like a simple question of who would finish him off first, the Mushin or the sword.

There was no way, he realized bitterly, that he could fight them both at the same time. If he removed his concentration for even the barest moment from his mental defenses, the Mushin would destroy him utterly. But if he failed to pay close attention to the movement and menace of the Ronin's sword, he would just as surely perish.

Either way, he lost. There didn't seem to be any rational solution to his quandary. The problem seemed as insolvable as the little puzzles the Old Master had constantly posed to him.

The thought of the Master abruptly catapulted Jerome out of the Now and into memory. He was sitting once more with the old man, listening intently to words he didn't understand.

"Your mind must be constantly flowing. It can never 'stop'. The mind of a swordsman must be everywhere at once. If it is stopped in the hands, it cannot be in the feet. If it is stopped in your lower abdomen, it cannot be in your head. When your opponent senses that your mind is stopped in one place, he will attack you in another. Perhaps you will be able to shift your mind quickly to the new point. Perhaps not. Eventually, though, you will be too slow and you will die.

"A non-stopping mind is called the 'non-abiding mind.' It does not reside in one place. It is everywhere, flowing throughout the body. If the hands are needed, it is there. At the same time it is in the feet, so no shifting is necessary to use them. When your opponent attacks, your mind does not stop with his attack, does not stop in the part of the body being threatened, nor in the part defending. It all flows as one, turning aside the opponent's blow and directing it back to him, killing him with the very completion of the motion meant to destroy you.

"When the mind is 'non-abiding' in this sense it is also 'immovable' in the true sense. That means it is not disturbed by anything. A mind which stops at an idea or an object is disturbed by that idea or object. It becomes preoccupied with that idea or object, so much so that it moves with it and is taken over by it. A mind which stops attaches itself to the thing which stops it and hence is no longer immovable.

"What you must try to cultivate is a mind both non-abiding and immovable. It must be everywhere and hence be nowhere. It must flow and in its very movement be still."

As suddenly as he had departed, Jerome was back in the present, a mere moment after he had left it. With him he brought a flash of understanding, a new awareness of what the Master had meant.

In the present situation, he would be destroyed unless his mind was truly non-abiding and immovable. Mere calmness was not enough: the combination of the concentrated mental assault by the Mushin with the physical attack by the Ronin was simply too overpowering to be handled in the usual way. But if his mind was non-abiding, how could the Mushin find it? And it if was immovable, how could the Ronin defeat it?

With relief, and for the first time fully comprehending what he was doing, Jerome relaxed his mind, pushed aside all the barriers and walls he had built up over the years, and opened himself to the universe around him. Far from trying to hide from the Mushin or keep his mind calm, Jerome dissolved his sense of Self until it merged totally with all that was non-Self. Individuality vanished, emotions evaporated even beyond the point of stillness. Nothing remained for the Mushin to detect.

Instantly he was no longer fighting the Ronin in the usual sense of the word. That implied two opposed forces, a Self and an Other. In his current mental state, Jerome was beyond such differentiations and polarities. Instead, he had transcended to a realm where opposites ceased to exist, where all things became one and the Universe was truly a uni-verse. Now he and the Ronin formed a moving unit, a singularity, a whole. When the Ronin attacked, Jerome simply followed and completed the motion, finishing the circle and returning it to the source. As long as the swordsman moved in accordance with the harmony established between the two of them, he was safe. But once the Ronin broke that rhythm, once he failed to receive the energy he had sent forth and Jerome had returned to him, he was doomed. Not because of anything Jerome did, but rather because of what the Ronin did to *himself*, through the totally reflective medium that Jerome had become.

The Ronin attacked, striking for the head with an overhand blow. Without thought, simply following the motion of the killer to its logical end,

Jerome raised his own weapon vertically and slightly to one side. The other blade slid down his and off to the left, just missing his shoulder, cutting nothing more than air. Following the trajectory of his own sword, the young man continued his forward motion. His body was well inside the Ronin's circle of defense as the blade sliced through the killer's shoulder right at the base of the neck. The steel cut cleanly, through bone and flesh , almost slicing the victim in two as it left the body somewhere above the left hip. The tip barely touched the ground, then rose again in the same circular motion, continuing its path behind Jerome, flinging gouts of blood in an arc. Back around to the front it swooped, cleaned by the centrifugal force. Without so much as a pause, it found its scabbard and returned to rest.

Stepping over the body, Jcrome noted that the Mushin were feasting on the dying Ronin's terror. The observation passed through his mind naturally, cleanly—felt and released. It was simply the recognition of something that was. The thought, if such it could be called, did not go beyond the Reality of Now, did not engender a whole train of new thoughts that led one away from Reality itself.

As he walked on Jerome noted that the two remaining Ronin were approaching him from different directions. Apparently the Mushin, before they learned just how dangerous Jerome was, had dispatched the pair to separate points on the perimeter, in case there were other humans lurking about. In any event there was no way both of them could reach him simultaneously before he had passed through the lifeless band—though the nearer of them would certainly intercept him well within it. The third, since he could not arrive in time to take part in the coming battle, was headed for a point just within the perimeter where he would be in a position to bar Jerome's path should he defeat the other.

Both Jerome and the two remaining Ronin continued on their separately convergent courses until the first of the pair was between Jerome and the Arks, about ten yards from the intruder. The Ronin planted himself squarely, sword above his head and tilted slightly to the right in the traditional high on-guard position.

This one looked to be an even tougher opponent than the last. There seemed to be more awareness in his eyes. His stance, though classical, was relaxed and natural. Speed, he analyzed, this one has great speed. Once again, the only way to win was with a non-abiding, immovable mind.

Jerome stepped closer and drew his own sword, holding it in a middle guard postion. This time he wasn't surprised when the Ronin spoke. "Come no farther, man. It is forbidden for those of your race to come within the ring."

He was disturbed by the eerie similarity to his previous encounter. Though the voice itself was different, it had the same flat, lifeless quality as that of the first Ronin. There was an awkwardness in the formation of the sounds that made Jerome wonder who or what was manipulating the mechanisms of speech. The Mushin? Were they capable of such things?

The Ronin stepped forward five paces and repeated his warning. Jerome held his ground. The guardian was obviously trying to force him out of the ring. He stepped forward again. Jerome waited.

With incredible swiftness, the Ronin struck, not for the head, but for Jerome's wrists. Jerome pulled his hands back, his elbows going out, shortening his circle of defense. The blow missed by a fraction of an inch.

Pressing the advantage presented by Jerome's shallower defense area, the guard stepped in, and thrust for the throat. Jerome parried the thrust and his blade flicked out like a snake's tongue towards his opponent's face. The Ronin responded by blocking upwards and Jerome circled beneath in a quick twist and went for the throat.

The guard's blade swept down, barely blocking in time. He back-pedaled in retreat. Jerome stepped in now, aiming two swift blows at the sentinel's head. The man blocked both cleanly, then sent a swift sweep toward the ribs. Jerome blocked and counter-thrust for the throat. Again the Ronin parried and back-pedaled.

There was something strange about the way the Ronin retreated so readily before successive throat thrusts; no swordsman this good would have so obvious a weakness in his defense. Jerome sensed a trap, decided to spring it.

He waited for an opening. Suddenly, too simply, too obviously, it was there. Jerome went in. As soon as he appeared to be committed, at the point where his blade had penetrated his opponent's defense—the point which the Ronin had back-stepped in the past—the guard twisted to the side, lashing out at Jerome's wrists, while Jerome's thrust met empty air. Had the Ronin's opponent been an ordinary swordsman the ruse would have worked to perfection. But rather than checking and pulling back Jerome continued his motion: with a sweep he was past and the man's blow fell in turn on emptiness.

As Jerome stepped past, the guard turned to meet him. His sword committed to the downward stroke he attempted to reverse directions and bring his blade back to guard. He was too slow. Jerome continued his turn, his outthrust sword describing a whistling arc around his pivoting body. The steel bit into the Ronin's neck before the man could raise his sword high enough to block. The headless, spurting body collapsed at Jerome's feet. A few feet away the head itself chattered momentarily in the dust.

Only one more guard remained between Jerome and the Arks. The last Ronin stood quietly waiting, utterly alert. No warning came from his lips, no forced mechanical words.

This one is different, Jerome thought wearily.

Simultaneously he realized two things. First, he was physically exhausted. The strain of two fights in quick succession, the second against a very difficult opponent, had been telling. I will be slower, he admitted to himself. And this man is faster. Second, his state of non-abiding, immovable mind was beginning to fade. Like everything else, he suspected, such mental states became easier with practice: At first the mind would fall back into its old patterns after a short while. In fact, it was rather remarkable he had been able to maintain it for as long as he had.

If his mind and body failed him at the same time, it was all over. The battering of the Mushin and slashing of the Ronin were too much for a fully rested man, much less a weary one. He shrugged and stepped forward. Nothing for it but to try.

One more step and the two swordsmen were within range of each other. Still the Ronin waited, calmly, his blade held lightly in mid-guard position. For a few heartbeats the two stood looking at each other in unfeigned interest. Then it hit Jerome. He isn't going to attack! He's waiting for me to begin. This one's a true Swordsman!

Shaken, Jerome took a step backward. The Ronin moved forward. With a growing sense of worry, Jerome feinted toward the head. The Ronin blocked casually, as if he had known the move was only a feint.

I haven't much time left, Jerome thought, realizing that the very fact he could think it proved how swiftly his mental state was reverting to normal. And the Ronin knows it. I've got to win swiftly or the Mushin will have me.

Committing himself to a course of action he had been taught to avoid, Jerome opened the assault. In rapid succession he aimed two cuts to the head, followed by a slash at the wrists, a blow to the ribs, and a quick thrust to the throat. The Ronin calmly blocked them all without even bothering to counterattack.

Mystified, Jerome stepped back for a second. No counterattack? Incredible! Again he leapt forward. Slashing and twisting, he tried to penetrate the man's defenses, to force him to give ground, to counter. He met with nothing but a perfect, unyielding defense. The guard wouldn't commit himself to any attack Jerome could take advantage of.

Jerome began to sense the bitter taste of defeat. The man would not yield, would not counter, would give him nothing to work on. It was like fighting a mirror-image. Wherever he stuck, the other simply blocked. The Ronin mimicked his every motion.

And waited. Waited for exhaustion of body and mind to bring his opponent crashing down into defeat and Madness.

I've got to win! I must win! he challenged himself. Ribaud and the others are depending on me! In a fury of growing despair, he launched into a third assault.

It was as ineffective as the first two.

It's like fighting myself, he thought wearily. Everything I do, he just copies and blocks. In the end, I'll be defeated by myself.

Wait! Like fighting myself! Of course! He knew his mental state was deteriorating. The Mushin must know it too. His trained, conscious mind was once more taking control and in all likelihood the mind leeches could sense it.

Perhaps he *was* fighting himself! If his actions, especially since he was attacking, were coming more from the rational, planning part of his mind, it might just be possible that the Mushin were able to pick them up. Since they were no longer coming from the non-abiding, immovable mind, there would be a time lag between their inception and the necessary nervous and muscular commands required to execute them. In that lag, the Mushin might be capable of feeding his mental state into and through the mind of the Ronin, much the way they feed a person's emotions back into his own mind!

Jerome tried a few feints. The Ronin responded just enough to match the seriousness of the moves! And the way he moved! With a sense of awe, Jerome realized he was watching himself!

The Mushin, he now knew, were greater, more devious enemies than anyone had ever suspected. Ribaud's worries over their possible intention of destroying the Free Brotherhoods no longer seemed fanciful.

Realizing his danger didn't solve his problem. He feverently wished there were some way he could warn Ribaud and the others, some way to communicate this ultimate confirmation of the Mushin's intelligence. But he knew that it was hopeless; he was totally alone, and soon he would be dead. His limbs felt like lead and his mind was numb.

Can't hold out much longer. I did so want to succeed.

"Desire is the most dangerous feeling that can inhabit the Swordsman's mind. Especially desire to win. But other desires are equally dangerous. Such as desire for good techniques.

233

Desire for perfect form. Desire to strike truly and cleanly.

"These desires, of which Swordsmen are especially guilty, force the mind to become fixed on an idea, to move with that idea, away from Reality and Now. When you are hungry, eat. When you are thirsty, drink. When tired, sleep. This is good. It is living without Desire. But . . . if you must have a fine, well-seasoned roast to eat, or must drink an excellent vintage, or sleep only in a soft bed well covered with a down comforter . . . ah, that is Desire creeping in. Suddenly the Nowness and Reality of hunger, thirst, and weariness are complicated with a thousand little schemes and desires and the trueness of existence is lost in the dreams of wish-fulfillment.

"A True Swordsman, one who would truly follow the Way of the Sword, must rid himself of desire to win. He must shed his desire for techniques and simply forget everything he has learned. Clean, naked, pure he must enter the world of Now. And ultimately he must shed even his sword. Only thus can he hope to hold the Sword that is No-Sword, the Sword sharp enough to cut Nothing."

Humbly, from the depths of his being, Jerome thanked the Old Master. "I understand," he told the air.

He dropped his sword.

The Ronin instantly went rigid, his eyes wide with surprise. Dumbly, he looked at his own sword, his grip loosening, about to let it fall to the ground. Then, with a great wrench of his will, the guardian reverted to his true form. He launched himself at Jerome, sword high for the death blow.

As the sword swept downward, Jerome stepped in and slightly to the left. His arms went up at about a 45 degree angle from his shoulders so that the back of this right hand touched the Ronin's arm at about the elbow. With this one swift move, he was within the guard's circle of defense and away from the peril of the descending blade.

Pivoting now on his left foot, he brought both his hands down, following the motion of the attacker. The left hand went to the man's neck, the right stayed at the forearm between the elbow and wrist. Turning to move in the same direction as the Ronin, Jerome continued the motion, the weight of his body forcing the man lower and lower. The swordsman hit the dirt on his face, his sword arm stretched out, his wrist held by Jerome. With a simple twist, the young man took the sword from his hand and threw it out of reach. The Ronin did not move. From the awkward angle of his head, Jerome realized the man's neck had broken as he hit the ground.

Rising, he walked calmly out of the lifeless area and into the green. He had reached Base Camp. As he stepped onto the grass, his weariness towered over him like a huge wave. Another step and the wave broke, crashing down.

CHAPTER XVII

HOURS LATER, SOMEWHAT refreshed by his sleep, Jerome awoke to the moonslit Kensho night. Two of the shining orbs were just setting behind the hills to the west. A third was at that very moment rising over the sea to the east. The fourth was still beneath the planet.

Since there was sufficient light to search by, Jerome decided to rummage about the ruins of Base Camp and see if he could find anything of interest. Wandering over the grass-covered mounds that were all that remained of the partially constructed camp, he began to realize there was one roadblock to his mission which no one seemed to have thought of. Ribaud had hoped his medallion would give him access to the Arks.

That was fine as far as it went. But how was he going to get *to* the Arks? The giant ships that had carried the Pilgrims across the vast wastes between Earth and Kensho couldn't stand the stresses of a planetary touch-down. They had been built for a gravity-free environment and would have disintegrated under the strain of climbing down the gravity well to the surface. The Pilgrims themselves had glided down in the one-way transports, now semi-dismantled and incapable of rising into orbit in any case. The heavy shuttles that had carried load after load of cargo down to the Camp had suffered a good deal of damage when the Pilgrims had been infected by the Madness. Now they stood, off to the left, rusting and falling into ruin. Yet they seemed to be the only hope he had of reaching the Arks. From where Jerome stood, they seemed a slim hope at best.

After a few more moments of peering at corroded and shattered bits and pieces of the Camp Jerome decided there was nothing there. If anything was to be accomplished, it would have to be done among the towering hulks of the shuttles. He abandoned his search among the ruins and headed out across the grass toward the ships.

There were perhaps a dozen of them, spaced evenly in two lines. The closer he got, the lower his hopes sank. They were wrecks, derelicts, probably incapable of any movement other than that of crumbling to the ground.

As he came around the end of the closest line and entered the alleyway between them, however, he noticed something strange. At the far end of the two lines, midway from either, was a form unlike that of the shuttles. From this distance he couldn't make it out too clearly, since only one moon was left in the sky. As he approached, the vague mass began to take on definition.

It was considerably smaller than the shuttles, and while the big ships were tall and cylindrical, coming to a point at their noses, this one, if indeed a ship, was shaped more like a flattened sphere.

The most startling difference wasn't revealed until he stood next to the strange bulk. Unlike the shuttles, it was smooth, unbroken, uncorroded, of a pure black color that absorbed rather than reflected the light of the moon. Jerome circled the thing, almost certain that he had discovered a vehicle that might carry him to the Arks.

He completed one circuit without finding anything that remotely resembled an access point. No doors or windows appeared in the hull. It was completely smooth and slightly warm to the touch. The second time around he noticed a slight indentation at about chest height. Curious, not remembering having seen it the first time, he walked over to it.

It was a rectangular depression, about two and a half inches long by an inch wide. He examined the edges with his fingers, pressed the center, tried to move it or make it do something. Nothing happened.

Carefully now, he circled the hull once more. Nothing. Not so much as a scratch anywhere else. Arriving back at the depression once more, he stood gazing at it. Absently, he began to play with the medallion that hung about his neck. During the fighting it had come out from beneath his robe.

He stopped with a start and looked down at the medallion. Ribaud had said something about it being an identity tag for one of the original crew members. Jerome hadn't completely understood what the old Sword Master had been talking about. But one thing he did realize: the medallion was almost identically the size of the depression!

His heart pounding with excitement Jerome lifted the medallion from around his neck. Then he unclasped the crude chain it was on and held it up to the depression. It fit perfectly, with an audible "click."

Jerome felt, rather than heard, a humming. Before he could locate it, the wall in front of him opened without warning. One moment it was there, solid and opaque. The next it was gone, in its place a corridor portal. A yellowish light filled the corridor within.

Hesitating, unsure, but seeing no alternative, Jerome entered. As he crossed the threshhold, he noticed how soft and resilient the floor of the corridor felt. It seemed solid to the eye, but yielded gently to his weight. A tingling at the back of his neck warned him that the door had closed behind him. Turning, he saw it was so. Next to the door, in exactly the same position as it had been on the outside, was a rectangular depression identical to the first. In it was his medallion. Reaching out, he retrieved it, carefully placing it once more on its chain, and slipped it under his robe. He felt a sense of security, certain it would let him out as easily as it had let him in.

Turning back to the corridor again, he began to

walk into the center of the ship. It has to be a ship, he told himself. What else could it be?

The corridor ended in a door which opened at his approach, allowing him to enter a circular room. Around the outer edge of the room were several rows of deeply padded, form-fitting chairs, about twenty-five of them. The center of the room was taken up by a cloudy translucent cylinder, perhaps ten feet in diameter, that reached from floor to ceiling. It was hard and cool to the touch. Peering into it, he had the impression that its depth was far greater than ten feet. Intrigued, he circled it once before taking a chair in the row nearest it.

Chairs were not common on Kensho; Jerome had some difficulty in sitting in this one. His tendency was more toward "perching" than sitting, for he was used to kneeling or resting on a cushion with his legs folded. Trying to adopt the same position on the cushion of the chair, he found his feet restricted by the chair back if he knelt on the seat cushion, and his knees hemmed in by the chair arms when he crossed his legs in the usual manner. He finally settled down, one leg folded properly, the other hanging off the edge of the chair at the knee. It wasn't very comfortable, he reflected, and it would be difficult to rise in a hurry, or roll away from a blow.

As soon as he stopped moving, the light in the room dimmed, and the cylinder began to glow. Suddenly, the cloudiness was replaced by the standing figure of a man, strangely dressed in form-fitting green cloth.

Startled, Jerome rose from his seat. The man

nodded his head in a sort of abbreviated bow. Jerome returned the greeting, never taking his eyes from the green-clad figure. His swift appraisal discerned no recognizable weapons, but caution was still in order whenever one faced a totally unknown opponent. Silently he cursed himself for a fool for having failed to retrieve his sword before entering the ship.

The man in green spoke, his voice firm and well-modulated, but with strange accent. The language was, however, comprehensible. "Estimated D-time: 04:37:19. Estimated A-time: 05:14:53. All systems ok-Norm. Field distort 005A2delta 8^2. Maint suggs recal. Any orders, sir?"

"Uh, no," responded Jerome uncertainly. "Uh, is the, ummm, ship moving?" he asked, hoping to gather more infomation without sounding too foolish.

"Current v .6 norm, .02 opt, rel v .000002c, max v est. .8 norm. Anything else, sir?"

Feeling bolder, Jerome responded, "Yes. Where are we going?"

"A-point desig Admiral's launch port 3, sir. Would you care for visualization?"

"Yes," nodded Jerome.

As suddenly as he had appeared, the man in green vanished, leaving in his place a sight that caused Jerome to stagger backwards and grab the arms of his chair for support. At the base of the cylinder, the floor had disappeared. At its top, the ceiling was gone. Below him, Jerome saw a vast depth, and at its bottom, what he took to be the coastline he had so recently been standing on. Despite the fact it had been night when he had entered, he could see the Sea, the Plain, the Waters, even the Mountains. White patches made the ground obscure in some places. He reasoned those were clouds seen from above. The view upwards was just as shocking. Off in one direction he saw the two moons that had already set, and everywhere stars such as he had never seen before. The sun was not immediately evident, but it soon began to move into view from behind Kensho.

Stunned and dazzled by the beauty of it all, Jerome quietly took up his position on the chair again. Behind his sense of awe, however, was a nagging wonder that the creators of such incredible things as this could be brought low so quickly by invisible creatures with no machines and no technology. A doubt was born in his mind as to the possibility of fulfilling Ribaud's fond hopes.

With unexpected suddenness, the Arks appeared above. Surprisingly, however, the ship passed them by. Suddenly a fifth craft was evident, though its presence was revealed primarily by the hole it created by occluding the stars in one part of the heavens.

As he drew closer, and began to be able to appreciate the true size of the ship, he realized that this must be none other than Nakamura's Flagship, the Mushima! Increasing awe filled him as his little craft floated gently into its berth within the mammoth cavern that was apparently "Admiral's launch port 3."

The lights in the chamber came up again and the man in green reappeared inside the cylinder. "Admiral requests your presence, soonest, sir."

Jerome hesitated. "Uh, fine. But, uh, how do I find the Admiral?"

"Just follow the blue line on the companionway deck, sir. Any further questions, sir?"

"No," he replied. But he really wanted to ask how a man who had been dead for at least 200 years could request his presence. For whom else could the man in green be referring to but Admiral Nakamura? And who was the man in green?

Shaking his head in wonderment, Jerome left the launch, entered the companionway, and followed the glowing blue line. He passed through several of the automatically opening doors, walked down the gently lit companionways, and even spent a few moments in a strange room which appeared to be empty and bare of all adornment except for a few flashing lights. He entered it, the door behind him closed, then opened again a few moments later when he stood before it. He walked out again, still pursuing the blue line.

Eventually, a final door disappeared in front of him, and he found himself in a huge, comfortably furnished room. One entire wall was filled with bank on bank of instruments and readout devices, none of which meant anything to Jerome. The wall next to it was transparent and yielded a breathtaking view of Kensho, all four of its moons, and deep in the distance, its bluish-white sun. Jerome walked over to it and gingerly touched it, just to reassure himself that there really was some kind of barrier between himself and all that immensity. The third wall, containing the door through which he had entered, was marked with a huge emblem in gold. It meant nothing to Jerome, but he assumed it must have held some importance to whomever had originally inhabited the room since it was so prominent. The final wall was blank except for a tiny scroll he couldn't make out from where he stood. Beneath the scroll, on the floor, were what appeared to be a zafu and zabuton.

"You're not Phillip Rausch, that much is certain," said a quiet voice.

Jerome whirled. There was no one behind him. His gaze darted about the room. No one. Not even a shadow.

"No, not Phil. But your genetic structure shows you're related to Rausch, though there's been drift. . . . . hmmmmmm . . . even mutation. . . ."

"Who are you?" Jerome forced firmness into his question. Invisible voices were no more terrifying than invisible mind leeches, he told himself. And if he could deal with the Mushin, then surely he could handle mere sounds. Yet he yearned for the reassuring weight of his sword in his sash.

"Who am I? No one, really. The man I represent is dead many years now. Or at least, so I surmise. His Life Force Indicators stopped transmitting some 235 Standard Years ago, just six Standard Days after he switched us to Passive Mode.

"Ah, but I'm not answering your question. You may not understand this, but I am a Simulated Personality Construct based on the personality of the late Admiral Yoshiro Nakamura, created by the ship's computer and based on the most recent data representing the state of the Admiral's mind as of . . . hmmmmmmmmm . . . not so recent, after all. Anyway, I'm as close as you'll ever come to the real thing now that the original is dead.

"My function was to substitute for the Admiral at times when he couldn't be available, due either to sleep cycles or conflicting duty. A Fleet Flagship must have a fully functional Master at all times, and no one man is big enough for the job. Subordinate officers may prove unequal to the task, hence there are always at least three of us SPC's for every crucial individual aboard a Flagship. Your distant relative, Phillip Rausch, as Chief Engineer, was, by the way, one such SPC'd individual. Would you care to talk to him? No? Hmmmmmmm, well then, perhaps you might be so kind as to tell me who you are?"

"I'm Jerome. Brother Jerome."

"Is 'Brother' your given or surname?"

"What do you mean? I'm called Brother Jerome or just Jerome. I'm a Seeker of the Way."

"Ahhhh. A Seeker of the Way. Which Way do you travel, Seeker?"

"Well, to be honest, I've traveled several," replied the Seeker. "I mean, I studied the Way of Passivity at the Brotherhood. But we all study that. Then I left and went to the Mountain to study the Way of the Sword with the Old Master. I left there to seek my own Way as a Wanderer. Now I'm here to seek a Way to save our race from the Mushin. I guess that's really been my goal all along, though. To find the Way mentioned in

Nakamura's Koan, the Way to free Mankind from the Mushin.''

"Excuse me a moment, Jerome," said the voice. "I see I am badly in need of an update."

Silence filled the room. Jerome looked around again, still half convinced there must be some origin point for the voice.

His search was interrupted by the return of the voice. "I'm back. Uh, would you prefer me to take a visible form, Jerome? I can project a holographic image of this SPC anywhere within the ship. Unless you touch it, you'd never know it isn't solid flesh and blood."

"Yes. I think I'd like that. I find it a little disturbing to talk to nothing."

"Fine. Let's see. I have a choice of wardrobes, but I think you'd be most comfortable with a Nakamura dressed in the robes of a Master of the Universal Way of Zen. So."

The door through which he had entered opened and slight figure walked into the room. With a light, springy step he passed swiftly over to Jerome and stood gazing at him. He seemed old, but alert, quick, in full control of all his faculties. His face was wrinkled, yet the lines said he smiled more often than he frowned. There was a twinkle in his eye that reminded Jerome of the Old Master and he could sense the laughter that lurked in the old man's throat. The robe he wore was as simple as Jerome's, though of a finer fabric. Jerome shook his head. It was hard to believe this was not a real man, the real Nakamura.

Nakamura nodded at Jerome, as if satisfied with

what he saw in the man who stood before him. Then he bowed his head slightly, a sardonic smile on his lips. "I am Nakamura. Or as close to Nakamura as is possible. At your service, Seeker."

Jerome bowed back. With a wave, Nakamura ushered him over toward the center of the room. "Seating, please," he said to the air. "Yes, sir," responded the empty room. As Jerome watched, two cushions and a low table appeared out of the floor. "Appropriate?" queried the old man.

The younger man nodded. "Easier than the seating in the ship that brought me here," he said with a smile.

When the two of them had settled down on opposite sides of the table, Nakamura spoke. "So. To business. I have reviewed the available data covering the period from the Admiral's death to your arrival at the Flagship. Sadly enough, several of the sensors and recording devices began failing some eighty years ago. Since the ship was in Passive Mode, no maintenance was performed and a great deal of data simply wasn't kept up to date. In any case, the value of such data is limited both by the circumscribed range of the instruments and by its passive, objective, mechanical nature. What I need now are active, subjective, human observations. So I'd be much obliged if you'd give me a brief update on the situation of the Pilgrims on this planet. It would help fill the gaps in my own information and make analysis easier."

For the next hour, Jerome repeated the history he had been taught in the Brotherhood. He told of the landing at First Touch, the Madness, the coming of the Grandfathers, the creation of the Way of Passivity. The little man sitting opposite him was especially interested in his accounting of the origins of the Way, and appeared most amused when told the Grandfathers had taken it from his own brain.

"Absurd," he chuckled. "Oh, on the surface it appears to be like the Universal Way of Zen. But the Universal Way never tried to repress or control Desire. Desire is to be ignored; once one gains a proper perspective on the nature of the Universe, it simply evaporated in irrelevancy. The Way of Passivity you speak of simply couldn't have originated in Nakamura's mind."

A second hour and a third, were spent in Nakamura grilling Jerome for details, demanding a complete recounting of his own life and experiences, his personal observations on what existence was like on Kensho with the Mushin hovering about, threatening to bring the Madness at the slightest slip. He was particularly rigorous in his request for a precise account of the apparent natural immunity Jerome, Tommy, Obie and Misako had to the Mushin. The description of the Old Master's antics and teaching techniques brought gales of appreciative laughter from the Admiral. And a recounting of Ribaud's worries over the fate of the Free Brotherhoods and Sisterhoods, and Jerome's subsequent mission to seek the weapon supposedly left behind by Nakamura, received grave nods.

But the thing he was most interested in by far

was the story of Chaka. The Zen Master probed deeply into every aspect of their relationship, demanding a detailed description of the girl's actions, manner of speech, attitudes, anything and everything Jerome could dredge up from his memory.

When he had finished, Jerome sat back, feeling as though Nakamura had physically wrung him dry of information. The old man had forced him to recall things he hadn't remembered in years. Details of the past that had seemed lost forever had become sharp as yesterday's sunlight under the probing questions of the quiet little Zen Master.

Glancing up, he noticed that the Admiral's gaze was intently focused on his hands. Looking downward, he realized he was fingering his Smoothstone and had been doing so for some time, perhaps since the very beginning of his narration. It was a silly habit he had never bothered to break. For some reason, it seemed to help him concentrate. Embarrassed by Nakamura's stare, he moved to put the object back into his pocket.

"Just a moment, Jerome," the old man interrupted his motion. "What is that thing?"

He held it out for inspection. "Just a Smoothstone," he said, a little surprised the Admiral didn't know about something so common.

Nakamura smiled at the proffered item. "No. I can't take it. It'd fall right through my hand. I'm only a light image. Please place it on the tabletop. You won't mind a slight scratch on it, will you? For sampling's sake?"

Jerome did as requested. Looking at the Smoothstone sitting there, the old man asked,

"Where did you find it? Are they generally dispersed or localized in distribution? Are they common? Rare? Tell me."

"Well, not common. But not rare, either. I mean, every kid goes out looking for one. Most everybody finds one, too. It may take a few years of searching. It's like . . . well . . . you've just got to have one, that's all." He shrugged helplessly at a loss to explain anything so simple and common. Thinking back, he added, "Come to think of it, I found mine at the base of a hill. I think that's the most usual place to find one."

"Hmmmmmm. Strange. Very strange. Analysis of the sample indicates your Smoothstone is a very complex type of cermet. To my knowledge, such things do not occur naturally. Nor did the Pilgrims have the industrial capacity, much less the opportunity, to manufacture anything of the sort. Hmmmm. At the base of hills. Every hill, or only certain hills?"

"Oh, only a very few hills. Maybe one in a hundred."

"Interesting," Nakamura muttered. "Excuse me Jerome, I have some very important correlations to run, sort of a giant multiple regression analysis. While I'm at it, I suggest you eat. I fear I've been a rather rude host, for which I hope you will excuse me." He clapped his hands. "Tea and rice, please." A voice from the air replied, "At once, sir." An instant later, the top of the table slid aside and a tray carrying a teapot, a cup, and a bowl of steaming rice appeared. "So. Please eat. The rice is fortified. It contains everything your body needs. Very convenient. The tea is also fortified. Most nourishing. Now I'll leave you to eat in peace.'' With that, the figure of Nakamura settled back into a meditation posture and froze in position, motionless.

Suddenly aware of his hunger, Jerome began to eat. It was a small meal, finished in a few moments. But it was satisfying and left him full and content. For a moment he wondered how the rice had been kept fresh for so long, then dismissed the thought. More of the Ancient's magic, he supposed.

No sooner had he finished than Nakamura stirred again and spoke. ''So, my friend, you have made a long and perilous journey, and you have succeeded in reaching your goal. As to achieving your purpose . . . that is, finding some weapon left here by Nakamaura to fight the Mushin, . . ahhh . . . that I cannot be so positive of.

''Quite simply, there is no such weapon. Think for a moment. Surely, if Nakamura had discovered such a thing as a method for defeating and killing the Mushin, the original Pilgrims and crew would have used it. None of this would ever have happened and you wouldn't be sitting here right now.

''No, Jerome, I'm sorry. But in all my data banks, I find not one shred of evidence that any help exists. If the Admiral had some plan, I fear it died with him. I can't offer you anything, weapon or Way, to save your people.''

CHAPTER XVIII

FOR SEVERAL MOMENTS Jerome sat staring gloomily at the tabletop. Then he lifted his gaze to the old man and whispered, "Then Nakamura's Koan is meaningless?"

"I've run enough semantic correlations on it to fill a good-sized library and still I can make no sense of it. Its meaning, if any, died with the Admiral, I fear."

"Then there is no Way to freedom? Mankind on Kensho is doomed?"

The Nakamura hologram looked up, startled. "Oh, my, no. No, indeed. Things never looked better!"

Totally bewildered, Jerome opened his mouth several times before he could find any words. "But . . . you said . . . I . . . don't understand."

The old man held up his hand and smiled. "Ahhh. I said I could not give you a weapon or a Way to fight the Mushin. By that I simply meant that I could offer no program, with tactics and strategy and so forth. And that is indeed the case: nothing of the sort exists. Fortunately, however, no such thing is necessary." The Admiral smiled again, a bit smugly, Jerome thought.

"Please, Master," he pleaded, "I'm very confused. Could you explain?"

The simulation nodded assent. "So. It's really no mystery, as I'm sure you'll see after I give you the first few pieces of the pattern. You have all the information yourself. It's just that you haven't organized it properly.

"You know how lethal the assault of the Mushin was at First Touch: my data banks indicate a kill-rate approaching 80%; since there were approximately 20,000 Piligrams and crew, that makes 16,000 dead. I estimate that another five to ten % were driven insane, or at least dysfunctionally disturbed, for a total effective kill of nearly 90%. That leaves approximately 2,000 functional individuals. Assuming that the kill-rate stayed relatively high for a couple of generations, then population regrowth must have been quite slow. The data you've given matches that kind of population curve very closely.

"Now a situation like the one I've described allows of only two alternative paths: rapid adaptation or equally swift extinction. Luckily, several factors were in favor of the former.

"First, the Mushin. They didn't want humanity

to become extinct. Hence the whole elaborate set-up: the Grandfathers, the Way of Passivity, the farmsteads, the Brother- and Sisterhoods, everything. And all of it focused on one purpose: assuring the survival of the food source.

"Second, my records indicate that basically two kinds of people survived the first Mushin attack: those who practiced some form of mind discipline, and those with unusually stable personalities. Thus, the 2,000 individuals who became the basis of the future population of Kensho started with a certain natural or acquired resistance to the mind leeches—or at least the ability to acquire it. That resistance isn't the same as immunity, in fact it aids the Mushin, but it has enabled humanity to survive.

"Third, a fact you couldn't know about. Kensho has a higher background radiation level than Earth and, as a result, the mutation rate here is higher. Of course, that means a lot more harmful mutations, but given the stresses of this environment I doubt their carriers would live long enough to pass them on. On the other hand, a higher rate of favorable mutations, given the small size of the breeding population and the degree of resistance they started out with, would lead to a very rapid spread of beneficial changes. And given the fact that the Mushin are the major pressure against survival here, the most favorable changes would be those that relate to the development of a degree of natural immunity against them."

"Which makes the practice of Calling the best into the 'hoods, where they won't breed, all the more important," Jerome commented thoughtfully.

"Precisely," nodded Nakamura. "Precisely. You follow the argument exactly. The Brother- and Sisterhoods have not only helped the Mushin control the human population, they also played an important role in slowing down the development of immunity. But it's only a slowdown. Regardless of their meddling, the eventual result will be the same.

"There is a fourth factor to consider, perhaps the most important of all. The Mushin attacked man's most versatile, as well as most vulnerable, aspect: his mind. Even stripped of its technological extensions, the mind is a formidable weapon. And it's the only essential part of a man that he can change by himself through an act of sheer will.

"Jerome, I don't know how many men like your Old Master there are on Kensho, but he's an example of what I'm alluding to. His ability to withstand the Mushin derives solely from the conscious exercise of his own mental powers. Even though it isn't natural, it's a difference in kind from the mere resistance possessed by the first generation of survivors.

"Ribaud and the others who survived the Freeings are the next generation and are even further along in the growth of that resistance, but their conscious mental discipline was nowhere near as strong as the Old Master's; Ribaud is correct in thinking that the Free Brothers and Sisters might not survive a second assault.

"But you, Tommy, Misako, and Obie represent

the first signs of something truly new: a quantum jump from resistance to immunity. All of you have had it from childhood and it has saved all of you at crucial moments. You, of course, have added to it with your mental discipline by following the Way of the Sword. In any case, my correlations indicate that you and the three children are merely the beginning, the tip of the iceberg, so to speak. After all, a natural immuntiy to the depredations of the Mushin increases the likelihood that an individual will survive to breeding age and reproduce. A mutation of that kind was bound to surface sooner or later since it's so beneficial. As it spread, it'll continue to develop, becoming stronger and more complete. The result, unless I miss my guess, will be a new type, perhaps even a new sub-species, of human being. One you're already familiar with.''

''Familiar with?'' What do you mean?''

''I mean Chaka.'' Seeing the look on Jerome's face, Nakamura chuckled. ''Oh, I don't mean literally. You see, your friend was something of an anomaly; in a sense, she was a visitor from the future. My data indicate that she is the direction in which the human race on Kensho is heading. Someday, when the immune genes are fully developed and have permeated the population, everyone will be very much like her.'' The simulacra sighed. ''What a pity she had to die so young. Why, if she had lived to pass on her genes, she would literally have become the mother of a new race! But to die so uselessly, without any good reason, what a waste, what a waste.''

Jerome smiled briefly in memory and then pondered for a moment. "How long will it take for these changes, these mutations, to spread?"

"Oh, not long. I would estimate that in another ten or twelve generations immunity will be quite widely spread. So you see, it's as I said: there's no need for a weapon or a Way. Humanity is over the hump on Kensho. The future looks quite bright."

Speechless, Jerome merely stared at the hologram for a few moments. "Ten or twelve generations?" he finally managed to force out. "How many years is that?"

"Oh, three to four hundred years, give or take a few dozen," the image replied casually.

Suddenly, the absurdity of the situation struck Jerome. Gods, he thought, how ridiculous I must look! Sitting here, hanging on every word uttered by a machine that's trying to act like a man two hundred years dead! By now, it was obvious that although the hologram might look like a man and talk like a man, it didn't think or feel like a man. Rather, it didn't think or feel at all; it merely gathered, tabulated, compared, and correlated data. Then it estimated confidence levels and decided what was most probably the correct solution. For most problems, that would be more than sufficient, but for others it would be an excercise in futility: the simple fact of the matter was that for it anything beyond its sensors and its built-in logic didn't exist. There was no way it would ever be able to offer a solution to his race's dilemma. It hadn't found one when the crisis first took place and it wouldn't now; if the real Nakamura hadn't told it his plan, as far as it was concerned, no plan existed. I'll find no answers here, from this thing that talks like a man, Jerome realized. If a Way of salvation exists, I'll have to find it on my own.

Suddenly Jerome began to laugh both at his own foolishness and at the hologram's assurances. "Nothing to worry about! In a mere three to four hundred years we have a great future! Wonderful! Ribuad will be delighted!"

The old man smiled benevolently. "I'm glad you're so pleased, though I admit I fail to see what is so humorous. But then, PSC's aren't suppsed to have a sense of humor. Oh, I've got some standard jokes for certain occasions, but Nakamura wasn't much one for standard jokes. He seemed to prefer puns and plays on words. He especially enjoyed juxtapositioning contradictions and incongruities."

"Oh, really?" responded Jerome, becoming attentive once more. After all, the pseudo-Nakamura did have a good deal of useful information.

"Yes," continued the construct. "I'll give you an example. The Mushin."

"The Mushin?" queried Jerome, all attention again.

"The Mushin. Of course, Nakamura knew even less what they are than I do now. But he played an exquisite word joke with their name, nevertheless.

"You see, the creatures appear to be some sort of self-organized energy field. Since one of the basic laws of the Universe is that it takes energy to maintain an antientropic state, we can deduce that the Mushin require engergy to maintain their own coherence. That energy must come from outside their own systems, at least in the long run, since there can be no such thing as a self-energizing field. Emotive energy, being a form of bio-energy, appears to be a logical source of 'food.' And one must admit that the average human mind is a marvelous source of emotively generated bio-energy.

"When the creatures feed, however, they destroy the source as the result of the method they employ to increase the supply. Simplistically put, they drive a man out of his mind."

The hologram of the old man held up its hand. "I know this seems roundabout, but to appreciate the Admiral's joke, you do need this background.

"The second piece of information, the one that makes the pun clear, is the data you brought me regarding the creature's intelligence. My own correlations agree with your guess that they are an aggregate intelligence. Alone they are mindless. That is, a Mushin, as such, has no mind.

"Now you can appreciate the pun. 'Mushin', in the ancient Japanese language from Earth, means literally 'No Mind'. Do you See? The Creatures have no mind, hence he called them 'Mushin'. And the effect they have on men is that they leave them with 'no mind'. It's a double meaning. Very clever."

For a moment the Admiral's image paused and looked thoughtful. "Hmmmmmmm. I have just correlated another meaning. In Zen Buddhist thought, 'Mu-shin' refers to the mental state of 'No-Mind', a condition one had to achieve before Enlightenment is possible. I don't see what that has to do with the creatures, but I wouldn't put it past Nakamura to have included that meaning as well. A triple pun!

Jerome was struck by what the hologram had just said. Mu-shin was a mental state essential to Enlightenment? Could that mean anything? Of course it did! He could sense the significance of it. But for some reason it eluded him, hanging like a cloud at the edge of understanding. Important, his mind told him. Important.

The pseudo-Nakamura had continued talking. He picked up his thread of concentration in the middle of a sentence.

". . . so the Smoothstone gave me the clue."

"I'm sorry," Jerome interrupted. "I missed that. I apologize for not paying attention."

An annoyed expression crossed the old man's face, but it seemed out of place, as though borrowed from someone else. "I was speaking about the origin of the Mushin. I thought the information I've extrapolated from all the data I've collected over the last 200 years might be of interest to you."

"Certainly."

"Well, the Smoothstone was the key. No matter how I ran the data before that, I'd come up with impossible contradictions. Creatures like the Mushin could not evolve on a planet like Kensho. Frankly I can't see how they could evolve anywhere. Furthermore, there aren't any life forms higher than the reptiloids anywhere on the planet. Given the data registered by my sensors, warm-blooded live-bearers should be prevalent. There is no doubt that proper excavations would produce evidence of fossil mamaloids. Apparently the

Mushin wiped them out long ago, just as they nearly wiped out mankind.

"Which hints at the idea that the Mushin are not indigenous. But where did they come from? There isn't a viable system within 100 light years of here. If the Mushin could get that far they would have inundated the entire galaxy, including Earth.

"The Smoothstone, though . . . ahhhh . . . the Smoothstone. It's obviously the product of a very advanced technology. A rather strange technology, to be sure, not at all parallel to our own. It appears to be a vastly sophisticated form of molecular biology.

"So I ran an analysis on the hills. In the inhabited area of Kensho alone there are fourteen identical hills. Each has exactly the same diameter, the same curvature, the same height, and bears the same types of vegetation. One is not far from your parents' farmstead at Water Meeting. I'd wager that's where you found your little memento.

"Extensive excavation of the hill sites would be required before my sigma levels would reach much beyond 60% confidence, but I estimate that the hills are the remains of a civilization that existed on Kensho before we or the Mushin arrived on the scene. And I would further extrapolate that the extinction of that civilization would coincide with the appearance of the Mushin.

"Beyond that, I'm reluctant to project. But one thing seems possible, provided I widen my definitions to include alternatives currently below the 50% reliability range. I project, hesitantly, that the Mushin may have been created by the very civilization they destroyed."

Jerome nodded. Interesting—but hardly of use in the current situation. Something to be remembered for the future, something that gave a sense of perspective to the present, too. But not of any practical value . . . unless . . . Suddenly he sat bolt upright. "Does if follow that if the Mushin are artificial entities they might not be capable of reproducing themselves?"

"It does not *follow*, exactly," responded the Admiral, "but it is possible, definitely possible. Without more data I can say no more than that of course."

"The Ronin!" said Jerome, striking his palm with his fist.

The pseudo-Nakamura looked at him blankly.

"You said you need more data. Well, Chaka and I once arrived at the suspicion that the Ronin acted as a population control mechanism of some sort. But we couldn't figure out why the Mushin would want to control human numbers. It didn't make sense. After all, the more people, the more emotions and the more food.

"But if there are only a limited number of the creatures, there would undoubtedly be some optimum number of humans, beyond which control would become difficult, maybe even impossible. By keeping the population below that level, they could assure themselves of maintaining their hold on us. Hence the Ronin."

After a brief pause, the surrogate responded: "Yes, it correlates. There's a 78% confidence level even without further data."

"Which means," Jerome mused, "if we can break through the passes to the plains, we'd be free of them.

"Oh, they could follow, but for every one that did, that many more people left behind would be free. We'd win either way. The Ronin must be destroyed."

Jerome's mind was already back on the planet, planning. He stood. "Well," he began, "I think I'll be going back home again. I've a lot to tell Father Ribaud and the Free Brothers. Not what they're hoping to hear, of course, but something of interest nevertheless. Thank you for all the information."

The figure waved aside his thanks. "Think nothing of it. I have one further thing for you, though, before you return. I'm sure the real Nakamura wouldn't mind. Indeed, I estimate with a 95% level that he'd heartily approve. I notice you carry an empty scabbard."

Jerome nodded.

"I assume you have lost your sword or left it behind. Aha! I was right. Well, the Admiral left his sword behind when he went planetside for the last time. I think he'd want you to have it as the first Pilgrim to return. It's over there by the wall, right beneath the scroll." The hologram pointed at the blank wall where the zafu and zabuton were placed.

Walking over, Jerome noticed for the first time that a sword lay on the floor between the cushions and the wall. Kneeling down, he picked it up, feeling the heft of it, impressed by the workmanship of the scabbard. Slowly, savoring every glinting inch, he drew the blade out. Placing the scabbard on the cushions, he held the weapon, admiring its balance. Then he went through one of the basic katas Ribaud had taught him so long ago.

Thrill after thrill passed through his body. This was a sword! It was magnificient! It seemed to move without conscious command, as if it were part of his own anatomy, never exceeding or understating a technique. Finishing the kata, his heart full of joy, he turned and bowed deeply to the hologram. "Thank you," he said simply and sincerely.

Kneeling again, he reverently replaced the sword in its scabbard. Then he untied his own scabbard and replaced it with Nakamura's. As he stood, his eyes fell on the scroll hanging on the wall. Casually, he asked, "What's that on the wall? I can't read it."

"Ahhh," came the answer from behind him. "That is the Admiral's favorite Koan. The very one he achieved Satori with. It's very ancient, Japanese, done by a Zen monk."

"Really?" he replied still gazing at the alien letters. "Nakamura's favorite Koan? What does it say?"

"Let's see, hmmmmm. Roughly translated it reads, 'Show me the face that was yours before you were born.' "

"Oh." Jerome looked at the scroll quizzically, then shrugged and returned his attention to the magnificent blade. What craftmanship, he thought. After three hundred years it still shines like a mirror. Tilting the blade this way and that to better admire it, he suddenly caught the image of his face, utterly clear yet strangely distorted by the blade's curving surface. Ah! he thought smilingly, perhaps *that* is the face that was mine before I was born. . . . No, he realized, the humor drifting from his mind like a cloud, the image is not real, no more than is the reflection of a moon on still water real. Remove the image and the pool remains. Remove the face and the steel remains.

Shifting the focus of his eyes, he looked through the unreal image of his face to the steel beneath. Even the blade was not what it appeared at first glance. Within the smooth shine of its surface were slight textural marks caused by the working of the blade and the consistency of the metal. Deeper he looked, beyond the surface appearance, seeking essence. Suddenly his eyes penetrated the steel and at the same moment it dissolved, leaving him leaning over an abyss. Without warning, the bottom fell out of Jerome's world, his mind tumbled into Emptiness.

From everywhere thundered the words of Nakamura's Koan, reverberating through his being, shaking his past to pieces, knocking all knowledge out from under him. "Show me the face that was yours before you were born." Slowly, as it swirled around and around, it changed, ebbing and flowing, into another Koan he knew so well. ". . . follow the Way that leads to the place where he dwelt before he was born." Merging, the two became one, the one become All, and the All became each. The face that was his before he was born was No-Face. The place he dwelt before he was born was No-Place. He was what he was, what he always had been, what he always would be. He wasn't This or That or Both or Neither. Like an onion, he peeled through the layers of identity he had created for Himself— Son, Seeker, Swordsman—down, down to the kernel that was No-Kernel. He was. And for the first time, it was enough. He let his Self go, only to discover it didn't exist. Completely, deeply, he experienced Existence without any hindering ideas or conceptions or questions.

This was the meaning of Nakamura's Koan. This was the place where he was safe from the Mushin. The place that had always been there, just waiting for him to find it. When first I began my search, he mused, the trees were trees and the mountains, mountains. The further I wandered, the more I learned, the more confusing everything became; the trees were no longer trees and the mountains no longer mountains. Now I have arrived, and once again trees are trees and mountains, mountains.

His inner eye open for the first time, he saw the Way he was to travel. It stretched out before him. clear and wide and effortless. It was the path the Old Master and Chaka had tried to show him, but which he had been too blind to see.

He realized now that he had lived his life like some tiny insect crawling aimlessly across the face of a vast plain. Unable to see very far in any direction, he had collided with every obstacle in his way, climbing wearily over the hills and stumbling raggedly through the ravines. He had taken each as a random thing, meaningless and disconnected from the rest. No patterns had been visible from his viewpoint, so, like the pseudo-Nakamura itself, he had assumed none existed.

Now it was as though he had suddenly risen high into the sky above the plain. From his new position, he could view everything. Individual features merged and became systems, the particular relating to itself and to the general. Order emerged from chaos. And there, amidst it all, his Way ran clear. Now he knew it and would never lose sight of it again.

This is the way Chaka saw, he exulted. And the Old Master. This is what it means to be free, to flow, to act without acting.

A joy that was No-Joy suffused his being and he looked outward once more. Everything was the same. Everything was different. He gazed down at the sword stuck through his obi. He smiled. Here was the Sword that was No-Sword, the weapon sharp enough to cut Nothing. Undrawn, it was sure to defeat Mankind's most dreaded enemy.

Turning to the hologram, he bowed deeply. "I go now," he spoke softly, not wanting to rupture the peace of the moment. "I have much to do."

Nakamura bowed in return. "The launch is waiting. Just follow the blue line back."

"And you?" Jerome asked.

"Me? Oh, yes, you mean me, the Flagship. Well, I'll return to Passive Mode. I have no other instructions. I'm good for several millennia in Passive Mode." So saying, the image wavered and disappeared.

Jerome bowed again to the empty room. "Thank you," he said. Then, turning toward the door, he walked across the room and left.

EPILOGUE

HE WALKED THROUGH the late afternoon light, the sun warming his face. As he crested the hill, he could see the shining of the Waters in the far distance and the dim mark that was the Free Brotherhood. Outside it, What looked like every member of all nine Free Brother- and Sisterhoods plus a sprinkling of 'steaders from around the immediate area was heading toward him. Apparently the lad he had seen at the last farmstead was indeed fleet of foot. That, or else word of his coming had passed ahead of him even more swiftly than he had imagined.

All along his return route, people had been waiting, watching as he went by. Every 'stead had disgorged families who stood quietly, hopefully, expectantly. He had waved to them all with a broad smile and a reassuring nod as he strode toward his goal. Their return smiles and waves had been heartfelt and glad.

For a few moments he stopped at the top of the hill, looking back the way he had come. No sight of the Sea could be gained this far inland, but it still clung in his memory. Then his mind traveled upward and outward. The creature in the Flagship was just what he had expected Nakamura to be like—and yet was so wrong at the same time. He suspected that even the science of Earth had not been able to do more than create the shadow of True Being, that the Essence of Mind was beyond artifice, would always be beyond it.

To think that the pseudo-Nakamura had not understood such obvious things! To deny that the real Nakamura had left any weapon, any Way to free Mankind from the Mushin! To say that Nakamura's Koan was meaningless! Still, the shadow had been useful, for it had helped him clear up many things that had been obscure. But useful as a tool is useful.

He chuckled. The hologram had admitted it could make no sense of the Admiral's sense of humor, so it really wasn't any wonder it had misunderstood his greatest joke. Nakamura had played a colossal trick on the Mushin!

The idea had first come to him, vaguely and without any precision, when the Admiral's image had mentioned the 'other' meaning of the word 'Mushin', the meaning it couldn't 'correlate'. He hadn't comprehended it immediately either, but had instantly recognized its importance. Unconsciously, his mind had continued to worry at the problem, and slowly an idea had begun to take shape.

At first blush it seemed absurd. But as he began to appreciate the character of the real Nakamura, glimpsed in flashes through the medium of the SPC, the more plausible it became.

Nakamura had been seeking some way to save Mankind from the Mushin, some way to make sure the race survived on Kensho. Escape had been out of the question. There was simply no way and nowhere to run. So the Pilgrims had had to stay.

He chuckled again! How he would have loved to have known the real Nakamura! What a great joke!

The Mushin were intelligent in a limited sense, intelligent enough to realize a good thing when they saw it. And Humanity was a good thing!

But they hadn't been intelligent enough to figure out a way to preserve that good thing. A 90% kill-rate! That was really burning up one's resources!

So Nakamura had provided them with a method. The Way of Passivity. It offered everything they needed. They'd jumped at it.

For Nakamura knew that if Mankind survived it would eventually reach exactly the point it now was at. The Way of Passivity was apparently to the advantage of the Mushin. But it was also to the advantage of Humanity, since it gave time to gain the collective breath, time to regroup, to adapt, to survive. As a Buddhist, Nakamura had believed that all men had the Buddha Nature. That is, he had believed that all men contained perfectibility within themselves at every moment. All that was necessary was to realize that Buddha Nature. It was not a question of searching, merely one of opening the eye and seeing and accepting that which already was.

And the Admiral had known that sooner or later some man, somewhere, would discover that nature and become free of the Mushin. The Way of Passivity stood as a barrier to that discovery, but no more so than other beliefs had stood in the way throughout history. Eventually, someone always realized the Truth.

So the Way had been born. And with it had come hints of other things. For surely, the Way of the Fist, the Way of the Staff, and even the Way of the Sword, had been part of Nakamura's scheme from the very beginning. It was too much a whole for that not to be true.

But the biggest, most important hints had been the naming of the mind leeches and the posing of the Koan. As the hologram had pointed out, 'Mushin' meant 'No-Mind' and was a double pun on what the creatures were and what they did. But it was the third, misunderstood definition that held the key. 'Mu-shin' was the state one's mind had to achieve before Enlightenment was possible. And by naming the mind leeches thusly, Nakamura had been pointing to the idea that they would become the medium through which men could achieve the state of Mu-shin. For to escape the Mushin, one had to achieve Mu-shin, and the very existence of the mental pressure the Mushin exerted on the race was an incentive to the gaining of Mu-shin. The Mushin caused Mu-shin.

The Koan was the second hint. It instructed men to look for freedom from the Mushin in the place where they dwelt before they were born. That place was No-Place just as the face referred to in the Koan that hung in the Flagship was No-Face and the state of mind necessary to Enlightenment was No-Mind. Each simply meant that one had to transcend the realm of the particular and the general, that one had to go beyond the ego-centered view of a Universe divided into permanent, meaningful Subject-Object dichotomies. The Seeker must return to the original Mind, the pre-Self consciousness that allowed him to permeate and be All Things while still retaining his own integrity. Once this was achieved, the Seeker walked the Way that accomplished All Things by doing Nothing. Neither acting nor abstaining from Action, he could wield the Sword of No-Sword to cut the Nothing that was Everything.

He snorted. It was so obvious once you understood it. But the understanding had to come from within, since there was no way to describe it to another with words. Even the words Nakamura had used in his hints had been purposefully obscure, contradictory, and mysterious. He had used them to create a state of mind in which logic and rationality became frustrated and confused so that the Seeker had to make the necessary intuitive leap to gain their true meaning.

How had the Admiral done it? he wondered. How had he planted the idea of the Way of Passivity in the Mushin's mind? Perhaps he had opened his mind to the creatures, just enough to give them what he wanted them to have, and then had killed himself before they could discover any more. Possible. That would certainly explain the Grandfather's claim to have found Nakamura dying of an accident. And the Grandfathers, were they part of the scheme, something Nakamura had likewise suggested? Where had they come from? Had someone built them? Or were they simply skeletons of some long-gone life form that was ready to hand and hence used?

We'll never know the whole story, he thought. Perhaps it's best we don't. No sense in setting up some kind of Nakamura Cult. The Admiral did what he did to put us on our own so that we could solve our own problems, he realized. When a man comes to the point where he can understand what Nakamura did, he won't need to know how it was done. Better that way, he concluded. Don't do anyone's thinking for him.

Turning toward the sun, he began his briefly interrupted journey again. He noted that the crowd had covered about half the distance between himself and the Brotherhood. He still couldn't make out individuals, but he did not need to know that the leader was Ribaud.

They're eager to begin, he analyzed silently. They don't know what's expected of them yet, but they're ready. He sighed. So much, so much would be required of each and every man, woman, and child on Kensho before they would be free of the Mushin.

Of course, they could just wait four hundred

years, give or take a few dozen, for natural immunity to develop. He chuckled. Somehow, he didn't think they'd much care for that solution.

No, he told himself. They'd want to take the harder way, Nakamura's Way.

First, he thought, they'll have to clear the passes. That meant training the young men and women to fight the Ronin. And teaching them to do it with minds calm enough to withstand the attacks of the Mushin. No easy task, but something that the Way of the Sword could accomplish within a decade or less.

Once the passes were open, families would have to be sent out into the plains beyond the mountains. From there, free of the Mushin, they could expand to settle the entire planet.

But to keep the rest of the planet free of the mind leeches,—to keep them bottled up just as they had bottled up Mankind—some would have to remain behind. The Brotherhoods and Sisterhoods would have to be restructured to serve a new purpose: on the surface, they would seem the same; they would continue to feed the Mushin, keeping them happy and satiated. However, it would no longer be an unconscious act, yielding benefits solely to the invisible creatures. Instead, it would be a way to keep the mind leeches locked up in the same prison they had once kept Mankind in.

Those who stayed behind would be doing something else, too. In addition to freeing their brethren, they would be freeing themselves. The constant presence of the Mushin would make it possible for them to follow the Way of Nakamura's

Koan and achieve Mu-shin.

Further, if they married and had children, they'd be helping to develop and spread the natural immunity the pseudo-Nakamura had mentioned. Eventually, they'd create a new race, a race of Chakas.

He smiled. It was pleasant to think that someday every child born would, in a very real sense, be his and Chaka's. He knew the girl would find the idea amusing. And he also realized she had probably understood it long ago.

Of course, the Freeings would have to stop: the continued presence of the Grandfathers would be necessary. Oh, the Fathers and Mothers would be the real rulers of the 'hoods in the future, but the Grandfathers would be left in their places to keep the mind leeches fooled.

He returned his attention to the crowd, which by now was quite close. Every member of it was silent. Eager, hopeful looks were spread on every face. As he had surmised, Ribaud led them. He stopped and waited for them on the top of a small hill.

They halted about ten paces from him, forming a crescent around the height where he stood. Slowly, Ribaud approached, placed his hands on his shoulders and squeezed them in greeting. He returned the old man's gesture. Then Ribaud stepped back slightly and smiled.

"You've been to the Arks?"

He nodded. "Yes. To the Flagship itself." The crowd murmured in appreciation.

"And did you find anything there?"

"Yes. I talked to Nakamura." The murmur became one of awe and wonder.

Ribaud's excitement showed only in his eyes. "Did you get the weapon Nakamura left to fight the Mushin?"

"No." Dismay rippled from face to face.

"No?"

"There is no weapon."

"No weapon?" Ribaud repeated helplessly. His voice presaged the onset of a grief that was total. "You bring us no weapon?"

"There is no weapon," Jerome said again, positively. "Nakamura left nothing behind except this sword." He gestured to the scabbard thrust through his obi.

"Then we are doomed." The old man's shoulders and face slumped in defeat.

"Again, no." He smiled at Ribaud, including all the others with a wide sweep of his hands. "We are not doomed and I do not bring a weapon—at least not in the way you think of one.

"Instead," said the Way-Farer warmly, "I bring you a Way."

There are a lot more
where this one came from!

The MS READ-a-thon needs young readers!

Boys and girls between 6 and 14 can join the MS READ-a-thon and help find a cure for Multiple Sclerosis by reading books. And they get two rewards — the enjoyment of reading, and the great feeling that comes from helping others.

Parents and educators: For complete information call your local MS chapter, or call toll-free (800) 243-6000. Or mail the coupon below.

Kids can help, too!

Ursula K. Le Guin

Mack Reynolds